J- FICTION

J. FICTION

Two Hot Dogs
with Everything

PAUL HAVEN

Two Hot Dogs
with Everything

Illustrated by Tim Jessell

Random House New York

Text copyright © 2006 by Paul Haven
Illustrations copyright © 2006 by Tim Jessell

Published in the United States by Random House Children's Books,
a division of Random House, Inc., New York, and simultaneously in Canada
by Random House of Canada Limited, Toronto.

RANDOM HOUSE and colophon are registered trademarks of Random House, Inc.

www.randomhouse.com/kids

Educators and librarians, for a variety of teaching tools, visit us at
www.randomhouse.com/teachers

Library of Congress Cataloging-in-Publication Data
Haven, Paul.
Two hot dogs with everything / by Paul Haven ; illustrated by Tim Jessell. —
1st ed.   p.   cm.
SUMMARY: Although everyone credits him and his superstitions for the
Sluggers' first winning streak in 108 baseball seasons, eleven-year-old Danny
Gurkin believes that his discovery of a secret from the team's past may be the
real reason behind the ball club's success.
ISBN 0-375-83348-X (trade) — ISBN 0-375-93348-4 (lib. bdg.) —
ISBN 0-375-83349-8 (pbk.)
[1. Baseball—Fiction.   2. Chewing gum—Fiction.   3. Superstition—Fiction.
4. Humorous stories.]   I. Jessell, Tim, Ill.   II. Title.
PZ7.H2987Two   2006   [Fic]—dc22   2005008344

Printed in the United States of America   10 9 8 7 6 5 4 3 2   First Edition

To Vicky,
and to my parents

CONTENTS

Two Hot Dogs

with Everything

FIRST INNING

Two Hot Dogs with Everything

Danny Gurkin turned the corner on Midland Avenue and raced up Splotnick Street, carefully avoiding the cracks in the sidewalk and making sure to keep other pedestrians on his left as he sped past. It was 3:57, and he had just eight minutes left if he was going to make it home for the start of the Sluggers game. They were playing Oakland, and Danny's favorite pitcher, Sid Canova, was on the mound.

Danny always wore the same shirt when Canova was pitching: a bright red T-shirt that said EL SID on the back in big white letters.

When Danny got to the corner of Beacon and Drew,

the light began flashing DON'T WALK, so he rushed across the street, quickly hopping onto the curb on the opposite side before any cars passed him. With Canova on the mound, Danny had to be especially careful not to do anything that would jinx him, and letting cars pass you before you got to the other side of the street was a sure way to bring bad luck.

Actually, Danny had been doing a lot of things wrong that summer. Crossing the wrong fingers. Chewing food on the wrong side of his mouth. Sitting on the wrong side of the sofa while he watched the games. Danny was convinced he was the reason the Sluggers were sixteen games out of first place.

The rookie pitcher had a great fastball, and a curveball that made left-handers look as if they were swinging a candy cane, but he had blown a game just a week before when Danny accidentally left the window open in the bathroom while he was brushing his teeth. How could he have been so dumb? He knew it would jinx Canova, and it did!

Canova's curveball hadn't curved, his fastball hadn't popped, and the young pitcher was taken out after just a few innings, with the Sluggers trailing 11–3. Finchley Biggins, the Sluggers' manager, blamed Canova's performance on a stomach virus, but Danny knew better.

"Never leave a window open when a right-hander

is on the mound," Danny thought as he crossed Highland Avenue. Just six more blocks to go. Danny was not especially big for his age, with knobby knees and thin arms and a round, open face. Now he was scampering along on his short legs, hurtling himself through the busy street, a blur of red and white—the Sluggers' colors, of course—past families out for a summer stroll, teenagers holding hands, workmen carrying crates of fruit into the local shops.

And then suddenly, Danny stopped. Danny stopped so suddenly, in fact, that his baseball cap fell right off his head.

"The hot dogs!" Danny said, loudly enough to get a few stares from a group of elderly ladies.

Danny turned around and raced back the way he had come. It only took him a couple of minutes to reach Willie at his usual spot.

"Two hot dogs with everything!" Danny said as he neared the food stand.

"Hey, Danny, is there a game this afternoon?" asked the hot-dog man, who by now had learned Danny's routine. "You want extra sauerkraut on top for good luck?"

"No, Willie, not when a rookie is pitching," Danny explained. "Then you need extra onions."

"Hmm, I didn't know that," Willie said, fishing a second hot dog out of the murky water and smothering it with a little bit of sauerkraut and gobs of brown onion goop. "What would happen if I put mustard on it?"

"Mustard's cool. That won't jinx them," Danny said. He would have to eat the hot dogs on the run or he'd definitely miss the first pitch, and Danny Gurkin never missed the first pitch.

Danny paid and rushed up narrow Chorloff Street, where he lived on the fourth floor of a six-story redbrick building. It was 4:03. Danny took the steps two at a time and burst into his apartment to find his older brother, Max, and his mother sitting on the couch, already set to watch the game. Danny sat down just in time to see Canova deliver.

The pitch was a ball way up over the batter's head, but that wasn't important. At least Danny had made it.

The Curse of the Poisoned Pretzel

In the history of baseball, no team had tormented its fans with more gut-wrenching defeats and wasted promise than the Sluggers. And in the history of rooting for baseball, no fans had been more devoted than Sluggers fans. Every bad bounce, every lopsided trade, every bitter loss, all were stamped onto the hearts of Sluggers fans — decade after frustrating decade — until misfortune became a part of them. Any of them could reel off a list of the team's most famous failures. There were the Phantom Strikeout of 1907, the Snowed-Out Summer of 1934, the Triple-Play Tragedy of 1967. The first had broken the heart of Danny's great-grandfather Zechariah Gurkin, the second had crushed the spirit of his grandpa Ebenezer, and the third still brought tears to the eyes of Danny's parents, Harold and Lydia.

In fact, in the 108 years since an immigrant bubble-gum tycoon named Manchester E. Boddlebrooks founded the team, the Sluggers had won only one championship, and that was in their very first year. Even that glorious season, as Danny or any other Sluggers fan could tell you, was tainted by tragedy.

It all started in the smoky clubhouse after the Sluggers won the World Series. At the time, all the players wore baggy wool pants and very small caps on their heads, and the gentlemen in the stands wore fancy top hats and had pointy mustaches that curled up at the ends like bicycle handlebars. Nobody realized how silly they looked because it was so many years ago.

Boddlebrooks wasn't just any bubble-gum tycoon. He was the type of bubble-gum tycoon people noticed. He weighed nearly three hundred pounds and had big, bushy sideburns and a kind smile. More than anything else, Boddlebrooks loved baseball, and he loved owning the Sluggers. He handed out gum and sweets to the players after most games, and on weekends he even let them come to his mansion outside town. The mansion was painted all red, the color of Boddlebrooks's most popular flavor of gum, Winning-Streak Watermelon. It had a fountain in the back that spouted bubble-gum-flavored soda and a giant hot-air balloon that looked like the biggest bubble ever blown.

Everyone loved Boddlebrooks. Everyone, that is, except his younger brother, Skidmore.

Skidmore C. Boddlebrooks was thin and wiry. He always wore a black overcoat and hats that were slightly too big for him, so his eyes were hidden in shadow. In fact, nobody could ever remember seeing Skidmore Boddlebrooks's eyes at all. He gave everyone the creeps.

Why Skidmore hated his brother so much was anybody's guess, but most people thought it had something to do with the fact that he was violently allergic to bubble gum. Skidmore saw his brother's sweet, chewable candies as a personal insult. The fame and riches the gum brought Manchester made it even worse.

On the night the Sluggers won the championship, as Manchester and all his players were celebrating in the clubhouse, Skidmore crept up to his brother and pulled something out from beneath his jacket.

"Here, try this," Skidmore said, revealing an enormous doughy concoction. "It's a new snack food I've been working on. I call it a pretzel."

Now, Manchester was an educated man with a passion for junk food, so he was well aware that the pretzel had been invented more than a thousand years before by a lonely European monk named Ralph who had a lot of time on his hands. But he didn't want to embarrass his brother by pointing that out, and he had to admit, he had never seen a pretzel like the one Skidmore had concocted, as big as a man's face and oozing with mustard.

Years later, Skidmore's creation would become the standard ballpark pretzel, sold by screaming teenage vendors in every ballpark around the country. Every ballpark except one, that is. Out of respect, no pretzel has ever been sold at a Sluggers game because of what happened next.

"Hmm, what a strange idea," said Boddlebrooks, his eyes twinkling with excitement at the Sluggers' great victory.

But no sooner had he taken a bubble-gum-tycoon-sized bite out of the pretzel than Boddlebrooks raised his hands to his mouth, turned purple, and fell over dead, his enormous body crashing down on young Lou Smegny, the Sluggers' lanky star shortstop, who never played another game.

The incident came to be known as the Curse of the Poisoned Pretzel, though nobody could ever actually prove that the pretzel was poisoned. Police ruled that Manchester had simply choked on the bread. Skidmore insisted that he felt terrible about the tragedy and would make his pretzels even doughier in the future. But the rumors started almost at once. And they grew louder when Skidmore inherited the Sluggers and the rest of his bachelor brother's fortune.

No matter how Skidmore tried to win people over, nobody ever forgave him for giving his brother the suspicious snack. The Curse followed Skidmore wherever he went, and it certainly rubbed off on his team. From the moment Manchester Boddlebrooks choked on the world's first ballpark pretzel, the Sluggers began a string of failures never before seen by any team in any sport.

Over the next 107 years, the world saw the invention of the car and the plane and the radio and the television. Nations rose and fell. Man cured polio and created the Internet and even sent rockets into space. All this came to pass, but not once did the Sluggers win another championship.

Rooting for the Sluggers was like praying for peace on earth. It was a noble and worthy cause, but one nobody really believed would come to anything soon. In fact, a century of suffering had produced a collection of traits by which really serious Sluggers fans could be identified. Jittery and nervous and used to disappointment, Sluggers fans walked with their heads down, their eyes hidden behind the bills of their baseball caps. The older fans had sad eyes and faces made gray by a thousand ninth-inning collapses. Still, to be a Sluggers fan you also had to have hope, a conviction that someday the Sluggers would win again and the sun would shine and everything would be right with the world.

Someday they would win.

Just not today.

Nothing's Working

As Danny and his family sat in a row on the sofa watching the game, Canova threw another ball. And another. And another. The first Oakland Ogres player trotted to first base.

Danny moaned.

Max slammed his fist.

Mrs. Gurkin left the room.

Nothing worked. Canova walked the first three batters. The bases were loaded.

"What have I done wrong?" thought Danny. "I ate the hot dogs. I got here in time for the first pitch. I didn't step on a single crack in the sidewalk the entire way home! Why are they losing?"

Danny mulled over all his superstitions to see where he had slipped up. Slowly, his eyes began to focus on Max, who was reclining on the sofa with one leg thrown over the top cushions, his head lolling on the armrest like one of those bobble-head dolls they sometimes gave out at Sluggers games. Max already had begun to thumb through a car magazine, and he was listening to music in a headphone in just one ear.

"What?" said Max defensively, meeting Danny's stare.

"Pay attention to the game! Don't you see what's happening?" Danny spat. Older brothers could be so annoying. No ability to focus. Ever since Max had turned sixteen, he had become a liability.

Max had once been as into the Sluggers as Danny was. But these days he sometimes didn't even watch the games and spent half his time talking on the phone in his room. He had even begun to forget the names of some of the less important players, an embarrassment to any true Sluggers fan. Danny had read about people's brain cells dying as they got older, and it seemed the only explanation for Max.

"I'm not going to stare straight ahead at the TV for three hours just so I don't jinx the Sluggers," Max said. "They're in last place anyway."

"If you don't show them that you care, how are they gonna win?" said Danny.

"Danny, they can't even see me. They're on TV. I could be fast asleep for all they know!" Max said.

"No duh, Max. I know they can't see you. But they can sense you," said Danny. "If you don't try, they're never going to win!"

Canova gave up a couple of hits in quick succession,

and the Sluggers were down 3–0. Max rolled his eyes at Danny and reached for the phone. The team didn't have a chance. As Max chatted away to one of his friends, Danny tried everything to counter his brother's bad vibes—sitting upside down on the couch with his feet up against the wall, standing close to the screen and sucking in his stomach like a belly dancer, crossing his legs and holding his fingers together in little circles like a yoga master.

It was no use.

By the seventh inning, the score was 8–1. In the eighth, the camera panned down the line in the Sluggers' dugout, and most of the players seemed to have lost interest themselves. Two were reading magazines, and the third baseman, Chuck Sidewinder, was writing a letter. The manager, Finchley Biggins, was taking out his contact lenses and putting them in a little green dish that he had rested on his knee. He evidently didn't want to watch.

Danny's mother popped her head back in the room from time to time to see the score, but in the end she gave up. Max left the room too, leaving Danny to mourn in front of the television set alone. Another loss, another game out of first place.

Danny watched every pitch until the final out.

A Day at the Park

It had been a dismal summer, and now school was only two weeks away. Danny had spent most evenings watching the Sluggers, and most evenings they had lost. That was baseball's best and worst quality — it went on and on. Football was just on the weekends, and basketball a few times a week, but baseball was a constant companion, 162 games a year. It stayed with you and wouldn't leave you alone, day after day, season after season, gnawing at you until it twisted into every cranny of your brain. At least, that was how Danny felt. It gave him a headache.

During the day Danny found relief from the Sluggers by hanging out, shooting hoops, and shagging flies with Lucas Masterly and Molly Fitch.

On the morning after Sid Canova's collapse, Danny walked down to the basketball courts in Quincy Park, a few blocks from his house. On the way, he passed Willie the Hot Dog Man on the corner of Highland and Renseller. Willie was doling out an extra-long bratwurst to the long-haired guy from the video rental store down the street, music blaring from a small radio he had propped up with a couple of stale buns.

"Hey, Danny, I'm sorry about the game." Willie grinned as Danny approached. "Not enough onions? What do you think?"

Danny knew Willie didn't really believe in all of his superstitions, but he was polite enough to pretend, partly because Danny bought a lot of hot dogs with everything. He must have been Willie's best customer.

"Nah, it was my brother's fault," Danny said, recounting Max's crimes in vivid detail.

"Older brothers can be rough," said Willie. "Mine's in the slammer. Robbed a bank."

Danny had to admit Willie's brother sounded worse. A little worse anyway.

Danny bought two hot dogs and walked off to the park.

Quincy was the only park within walking distance of Danny's apartment, and on warm summer days it was always packed with kids from John J. Barnibus Middle School and Louis Canfield High School.

Louis Canfield was where Max went to school, and it was right down the street from John J. Barnibus.

Max spent a lot of time at Quincy Park too, but he would usually ignore Danny and stick with his friends. It was a rule of the street. Kids from the Can—as Canfield High was known—never talked to those from the John in public, even if they were related.

Quincy Park had one full court, but that was always taken by the bigger kids from Louis Canfield. Danny, Molly, and Lucas had to make do with one of the single baskets off to the side.

Molly and Lucas were in the middle of a game of horse when Danny arrived. He took a seat by the fence under the basket and popped the last bit of hot dog into his mouth.

"Bank shot, over the shoulder, nothing but net," Molly said as Lucas shook his head and scrunched his eyebrows.

Lucas was two inches shorter than Danny, with ruddy cheeks and big meaty arms. Some kids in the neighborhood suggested that he had a weight problem, but Lucas looked at it as more of a weight advantage. He was forty pounds better than everybody else.

"No chance, Mol. You got nothin'," he shouted as she lined up the shot. "Miss it!"

But Molly didn't miss. The ball clanked off the metal backboard and swished through the red hoop. Actually, it didn't swish because somebody had stolen the net. But it went through the basket without touching the rim all the same, just as Molly had called it.

"Looks like you're in a bit of trouble, Doughboy," Molly said.

Molly Fitch was the only person who could call Lucas Doughboy without getting socked. She was the tallest of the three friends and by far the best basketball player. She had straight red hair, freckles, and a high forehead that made her look extremely smart. Molly's father also had the coolest job of all of their parents, hands down—he was a sportswriter for the *Daily Bugler*.

He got free Sluggers tickets. Enough said.

Molly had been voted an honorary boy by Lucas and Danny when they were all six years old, and had kept the title even though earlier that summer she had been observed using nail polish, a troubling development.

As Molly strutted triumphantly toward Danny, Lucas ran down the ball and came back to get set for his shot. He had to heave it over his shoulder exactly as Molly had done or he'd pick up another letter and be up to *H-O-R-S*, one miss from losing the game.

He licked his index finger and put it in the air, pretending to get a read on which way the wind was blowing. He took three uncertain steps and flung the ball over his shoulder, but he was way too close to the basket.

Clank!

The ball banged off the rim and back into Lucas's body. His cheeks were even redder than usual as he brushed himself off.

"The game is a draw," Lucas said. "Danny's here now, so we should start over."

Lucas had a way of convincing you of something even if you knew it was ridiculous, and Molly accepted the draw even though she was thrashing him.

Having a friend like Lucas could be a very good thing if you were on the scrawny side like Danny. He'd never been in an actual fistfight, but Lucas was a master of the angry stare that would make the other guy think twice. He had come to Danny's defense on more than one occasion.

Lucas was no bully, and he never picked on anyone who hadn't picked on him first, but he just couldn't stay out of trouble. Danny had figured out with a calculator one night that Lucas had been grounded for various offenses for approximately three of the five years they had known each other.

"Terrible game last night," Lucas snorted as he grabbed the ball from Molly and chucked it toward the basket. "Canova looked like he was pitching uphill."

"My dad said he saw him throwing up in the locker room after the game," Molly said, grabbing the rebound and dribbling it between her legs, then around her back. "Apparently he's afraid they're going to send him back to the minors."

"Wow!" said Lucas. "That's rough."

For Danny, the little tidbits of locker-room gossip Molly got from her father were like pennies from heaven. He would play them over in his head endlessly during the day until it was time for another game.

Danny tried to imagine what it would have been like to be the sad young pitcher. He felt responsible for the rookie's suffering.

"Sid Canova's future in the big leagues is the least of our worries," Molly said. "He may have gotten shellacked last night, but at least he doesn't have an entire year of Mrs. Sherman's history class staring him right in the face!"

Danny slouched and his stomach churned at the thought. It was getting harder and harder to ignore the fact that in fourteen days, thirteen hours, and six minutes the three of them would be sitting face to face with middle-school Armageddon.

Mrs. Sherman, known by generations of children at Barnibus as the Sherman Tank, was an unblinking woman who barked out commands as if she were addressing troops storming a mountain instead of kids trying to learn the ins and outs of American history. Max had been in her class five years earlier, and Danny could remember the long, vacant stares he came home with each afternoon, and the pages and pages of frantically completed homework he would leave the house with each morning.

Lucas had been pretending all summer that he couldn't care less about being in Mrs. Sherman's class, but Molly and Danny were both big enough to admit they were terrified. Even Danny's mother, who taught eighth-grade English at Barnibus, thought Mrs. Sherman was scary.

"I have a cunning plan for dealing with her," Lucas said, bouncing a shot off the rim.

"Go ahead, I'm all ears," said Danny.

"Well, I'll get her a gift on the very first day of class, and then after she likes me I'll just sit in the back of the room and not say anything the rest of the year."

"Don't you think other people have tried that before?" said Molly, sticking the basketball under her arm. "George Mincy's older brother brought Mrs. Sherman a box of chocolates on the first day of class three years ago, and he's *still* in her class. She's flunked him every year!"

"I don't believe you," said Lucas. "And anyway, I have a plan B."

"Which is . . . ?" said Danny.

"If she calls on me, I'll pretend to have laryngitis."

"Good plan!" said Danny with a laugh.

Molly was laughing too. She lined up a three-point shot and rattled it in.

Troubling News

Two days — and two Sluggers losses — later, Danny and Lucas were playing catch at Quincy Park when Molly came running over. Something was bothering her, and her hair was frizzed up as if she'd left the house in a hurry.

"I have to show you guys something," she said breathlessly, pulling a folded newspaper clipping out of her back pocket and spreading it out on the grass. Lucas ran over from the other side of the field and the three gathered round and took in the news.

BODDLEBROOKS MANSION TO BE CONDEMNED screamed the headline in the *West Bubble Eagle*, a small paper from out of town. Molly's father often got Sluggers news before anyone else, and when he did, he passed it on to Molly to share with her friends.

Lower down, the article read: *Rotting Bubble-Gum Building a Blight to Suburban Community—Residents Want It Removed to Make Way for Shopping Mall.*

Danny and Lucas were shocked.

"I've never even been there yet," mourned Danny. "They can't just tear it down. It's history!"

"There's got to be some kind of law against that," huffed Lucas. When Lucas got angry, he swayed from side to side and breathed out through his nose. He looked like he could totter either way, which had a tendency to make those around him nervous.

"My dad says there's nothing anybody can do to stop it. The West Bubble Town Council owns the land and the building because Skidmore Boddlebrooks had to turn it over to them when he lost his fortune," Molly said. "They can do whatever they want with it."

Danny had read about the mansion in books about the Sluggers' early days, but the building had been closed to the public for a decade pending repairs that the town council said it didn't have the money to complete. Danny desperately wanted to go.

The house had fifty-two bedrooms, one for each flavor of gum Boddlebrooks created. One room was said to hold a giant popcorn-popping machine for when Manchester threw his famous parties.

Then, of course, there was the backyard. Manchester had servants stick thousands of pieces of bubble gum to the branches of the trees so that guests could pick all his unusual flavors. There was a prize for whoever got the most.

After Manchester's death, Skidmore tried to sell the house, but he couldn't find anyone to take it. There weren't that many billionaires interested in a red fifty-two-bedroom mansion, especially one tainted by the Curse of the Poisoned Pretzel.

Still, nobody had had the heart to tear the place down — until now. For some time it had been a sort of pilgrimage for Sluggers fans, a place to relive the fleeting glory of that long-ago season. But the numbers of visitors dwindled year after year. After more than a century, many people had forgotten the mansion existed at all.

The article said the West Bubble Town Council had voted to bring the building down with explosives in what they referred to as a "controlled implosion."

Danny felt his temperature rise and an angry knot form in his stomach. It was like finding out that the Taj Mahal was being bulldozed to make room for a gas station.

There was also the matter of the Sluggers' slim play-off hopes. An act of desecration like this would surely hurt the team's cosmic vibes, and no number of crossed fingers or properly topped hot dogs could undo the damage.

"We've got to stop it," Danny said, his voice deeper than usual. Molly and Lucas looked up with surprise.

Danny had seen people on television chain themselves to trees to stop roads from being built, and others go on hunger strikes to protest this or that. Danny wasn't sure he was the tie-yourself-to-a-tree type of kid, and he certainly couldn't imagine going more than a few hours without eating. There had to be something he could do!

Danny stared at Molly and Lucas, and the look in his eyes said it all. They weren't going to let the town tear down that house.

Not without a fight.

Not without at least seeing the place first.

A Desperate Plan

"Why not!?" Danny cried when his father told him he was too busy to drive up to the mansion that weekend. Danny had launched what he thought was a gripping appeal—connecting with his father as a human being in need, a cherished offspring, and most importantly, a fellow Sluggers fan.

"The election is only two months away, Danny, and

things are way too busy in the office right now," said Harold Gurkin, gripping his morning coffee and flipping rapidly through the newspaper at the kitchen table. "I promise I can take you anywhere you want to go . . . after November."

"November! What good will that do?" Danny moaned.

Hadn't his father heard a word he was saying? The Boddlebrooks building would be a heap of rubble by then.

Danny's father was the campaign manager for Mayor Fred Frompovich, and he was suddenly a very busy man. Frompovich was behind in the polls, and it was Mr. Gurkin's job to get him reelected in November.

The mayor himself wasn't helping matters any.

Just three weeks earlier, Frompovich had been caught smoking in the backseat of a movie theater, even though his administration had pushed to ban smoking in public places.

At first, the mayor pretended he was carrying the cigarette for a friend and that it had spontaneously lit itself when his overcoat rubbed back and forth, but Frompovich's election opponent hired a physicist to prove that the story was impossible.

Soon other scientists joined in, and the consensus was that a cigarette could not light itself.

The newspaper tabloids loved the story.

FREDDY FRICTION CAUGHT IN FANTASTIC FIB! read one headline.

SPONTANEOUS COM-BUST-ED! screamed another.

Finally, the mayor was forced to go on television and tearfully admit he had lit the cigarette himself. He acknowledged he had a smoking problem and said he was going to deal with it with the help of his family, a spiritual adviser, and $29.95 worth of nicotine gum that a friend said just might work.

The scandal meant lots of late nights for Harold Gurkin, who was trying to get the campaign back "on message."

Danny didn't know what "on message" meant, but his father told him it had to do with economic growth and happy families.

The message evidently didn't extend to Mr. Gurkin's own family because correcting the mayor's missteps meant Danny's father had been too busy that summer to throw a baseball around, take Danny to the movies, or even watch the Sluggers.

"And I'm sorry, Danny, but there is definitely no time to take you kids out to that old house!" his father said, tapping his foot anxiously on the leg of the table.

What was happening to this family? Grandpa Ebenezer would spin in his grave if he could see how Danny's father and brother had abandoned the team.

Danny was sure Tornadoes fans never had these types of family issues.

The Tornadoes were in first place, as usual, a healthy seventeen games in front of the Sluggers. They didn't just beat teams. They crushed and humiliated them. They chewed them up and spat them out and left them quaking in misery. The team had won the last four World Series, and they looked to be marching toward a fifth title behind the ferocious pitching of Magnus Ruffian, a six-foot-eight Swede who grew up in a Nebraska prison, where his father was the warden. He was mean, and so were the Tornadoes.

Their fans' maniacal support never wavered for a second — as sure as fleas on a dog, as constant as homework, as powerful as a baseball in the nose.

It wasn't the desperate, nail-biting, toe-curling, scream-to-the-skies type of support Sluggers fans embraced. Tornadoes fans didn't need that, and they wasted no time on superstitions either.

They had money instead.

Tornadoes fans spent their days laughing loudly about a lifetime of championship seasons, lucky bounces, and stirring comebacks with the confidence of people who felt that success was bestowed on them from the heavens.

These people were not like Danny. They were different. They were happy.

They were from Texas.

The Tornadoes' history could not have been more different from that of the Sluggers. Even before their first game, in 1904, a worker breaking ground on the stadium put his shovel in the dry Texas soil and struck oil, sending a geyser of black liquid high into the sky. It took two weeks to bring it under control, and by then the dizzying stench of oil was everywhere. Rivers of it snaked away like trails of lava.

The team owner, a door-to-door saddle salesman named "Diamond" Bob Honeysuckle, was suddenly filthy rich.

Diamond Bob flaunted his newfound wealth, building an oil field right around the stadium and ringing it with giant pumps and drills. There were even oil pumps in the parking lot. The clank of machinery went on day and night, even when a game was on, a reminder to visitors that the team's wealth and power had no end.

When Danny was six years old, the Tornadoes stole away his favorite Sluggers player, shortstop Rocco Barnworthy, by buying him a private plane and promising him buckets of money and his own personal oil field. Barnworthy didn't hesitate to leave the Sluggers and sign on the dotted line. It was Danny's first hard lesson in how the world works, and it wasn't until he turned eight that he began to get over it.

Danny could see that beating the Tornadoes would take a miracle.

And the last time the Sluggers had had a miracle, people were riding horses to work and wearing funny hats.

Danny couldn't help thinking that it was because of people like Max, and now his father, that the team could never make good.

Danny hoped Lucas and Molly would have better luck convincing their parents to take them to the Boddlebrooks mansion, but when he met them down at the Quincy Park courts the next day, they'd come up empty.

"Our car is in the shop," said Lucas, his eyes darting to the ground. "My mother said it won't be in any shape to make the trip even after it's fixed."

Lucas's parents' car was always breaking down or catching on fire or getting a flat tire. It was a rusty blue 1978 Chevy Nova that Mr. Masterly called a classic but all the kids in the neighborhood considered an eyesore. Mr. Masterly was very proud of how long he'd kept it on the road, even if it did barely work and you could hear it coming a mile away. It was not something you wanted to tease Lucas about unless you were in the mood for some pain.

Lucas and Danny turned to Molly as their last hope.

"Don't look at me," she said. "My dad is going out

of town this weekend with Cheryl. I'm staying with my mother and she doesn't own a car."

Cheryl was Mr. Fitch's new girlfriend, and Molly was not particularly crazy about her. She was an interior decorator and had an annoying habit of changing everything she put her hands on, including Molly's dad.

"How about your mom?" Molly asked.

"She doesn't like to drive on the highway," Danny said.

The world was a deeply unfair place. Danny heaved the basketball at the rim in disgust and was surprised when it went straight in.

"We could always bike it," he said, and the fact that he'd hit the shot gave his words extra weight. Danny, Molly, and Lucas stood in silence for a few seconds as the idea floated between them.

"It's only about thirty miles. I think we could do it," Danny continued. "I printed out a map off the Internet last night."

"I would get *so* grounded if my parents knew I was biking out of town. It would be like a year before they let me out again," Lucas said.

Molly had some reservations too.

"Thirty miles is a long way. Do you really think we could make it?"

"I guess we won't know unless we try," said Danny.

"Well, if we do it, we have to come up with a good

cover story," said Lucas. He was clearly coming around to the idea. It offered the possibility of trouble, and something inside him just couldn't resist. "And we'll have to meet somewhere secret so nobody sees us together. We can't just set off from the park."

Molly bit her nails.

"So . . . let me get this straight," she said slowly. "We're going to lie to all of our parents. We're going to meet at a secret location, then ride our bikes to a town we've never been to before using a map printed out off the Internet. Then we're going to somehow save the Boddlebrooks mansion from being torn down, even though we really don't have a plan or anything. Then we are going to ride all the way back home, all before our parents notice we're missing. Is that what you're proposing, Danny?"

When you put it like that, it didn't sound like such a good idea, Danny thought. But he wasn't going to back down now.

"Yeah. That's the plan," he said.

There was a long pause as Molly's and Danny's eyes met.

"Well, I'm in!" she said with a smile.

SECOND INNING

Secret Rendezvous

At seven a.m. that Saturday, Danny, Molly, and Lucas met on Beatlechuck Street, about a quarter of a mile from Danny's apartment. It was a street that Danny hardly ever went to. It had a McDonald's, a gas station, and a car wash on it, but no residential buildings, and there were hardly any people on the street.

Danny was riding his blue T-150 Alibaba Racer. It had once been his brother's, but it was still in pretty good shape. Molly's bike was a green Cannondale R300 Roadster that was a birthday present from her father, one of the many great presents Molly got when Mr. Fitch was feeling guilty about the divorce. It was so light you could lift it over your head with one hand. Danny figured it was probably worth about the same amount as Mr. Masterly's old Chevy.

Lucas was riding a dented black contraption that looked like the bike the delivery guy from Mr. Chen's Chinese Takeout used. It was so old it seemed as if it might buckle under Lucas's weight at any time. Plus, it had a clunky metal basket in the front, the final indignity.

This was going to be an interesting trip, Danny thought.

Danny had the directions to West Bubble on a printout in his back pocket and a bottle of water in a backpack slung over his shoulder.

He had snuck into the kitchen the night before and made three tuna-and-pineapple sandwiches. He wasn't sure how they would taste, but it was all he could find in the fridge. They were wrapped in tinfoil and crammed into the front pouch of his backpack, along with a bicycle repair kit that Molly had brought along.

"Ready?" Danny asked, and Molly and Lucas nodded. The three were wearing Sluggers caps, and Danny had his Sid Canova T-shirt on as well.

"I told my parents I was going to hang out at Molly's place," said Lucas.

"My mother thinks I'm with Danny all day," said Molly.

As Danny raced out of the apartment that morning, he had told his mother he was going swimming with his two friends. Lydia Gurkin had kissed him on the cheek and told him to have fun.

On the ride to Beatlechuck Street, Danny thought about the story he'd told his mother. The lie had rolled off his tongue so much more easily than he'd thought it would. Sure, he had lied to his parents before, but mostly about little things. There was the time he'd used a painted Mexican platter his parents got on their honeymoon as first base and blamed it on Max when it broke. And the time he'd faked his father's signature and cut school to go to a baseball-card show and get Sid Canova's autograph. Then, of course, there was the time . . . Well, who had time for lists.

But the fact was he'd never made up a lie like this. Not one involving leaving the city limits. Not one that could land him on one of those reality television shows about police tracking down runaways.

Danny knew he was doing this for a good cause, and if things worked out as planned, his parents would never even know. Danny thought of Grandpa Ebenezer shivering in the bleachers in 1934, when the Sluggers were headed for a pennant until the first and only

August blizzard in history dumped ten feet of snow on the Sluggers' Winning Streak Stadium and washed out the rest of the season. If he were still alive, Grandpa Ebenezer would understand what Danny was doing.

"All right," Danny said, unfolding the map and pointing to a thin line that snaked off to the left of the city. "We can make it most of the way on the Sunshine Parkway, which starts over at Pikesmith Street."

Molly and Lucas huddled around the printout. Pikesmith was about twenty-five blocks away from where they were. It was hard to tell exactly because the map was kind of small and the ink was smudged.

"The only really tough spot is after that because we're going to have to go for a few miles on the Harry Tinkleford Highway," Danny said. "It's a really big highway, you know, with five lanes. But we only need to stay on it for three miles, and then we're nearly in West Bubble."

Danny looked at Molly and Lucas to see if he was losing them, but they seemed to be okay with the plan. Danny didn't want them to know that he was a tiny bit nervous about the highway part. He'd never seen anyone biking on the side of a highway before, let alone a trio of eleven-year-olds on a secret mission to save a baseball mansion. He could see that an outside observer, or, say, one of their parents, might think it was a stupid thing to do. They might even see it as something that merited being grounded . . . forever.

If Danny's calculations were correct, it would take about three hours of solid riding to get to West Bubble, assuming they didn't get lost. That would leave them three hours to look around and still be able to get back by four o'clock.

"Let's go!" said Lucas, and they put their fists together. Danny was also crossing his toes for good luck and silently repeating the words "West Bubble" in his brain. It just seemed like the thing to do.

Lucas was the first to kick off, his bike wobbling from side to side as he built up speed. Molly and Danny took off after him.

They pedaled through neighborhood streets buzzing with early-morning activity: a grocer stacking cucumbers and green peppers, a newspaper vendor cutting the string off a stack of fresh papers. Danny was beginning to get excited.

Those first ten minutes were pure elation.

The problems started during minute eleven.

A Trip to the Country

"Danny? Danny Gurkin! What are you kids up to so early in the morning?"

They were stopped at a red light on Pembroke

Street and the voice piercing the air like a gunshot was that of Mrs. Miliken, Danny's mom's aerobics instructor, who had just popped out of Leo's Bakery and was standing right behind them.

Disaster! They were already spotted.

Danny swiveled around on his bike and tried to smile, but his heart was in his stomach.

"Oh, hey, Mrs. Miliken. Yeah, we're . . . ah, we're just off to the park," he said.

"Oh, lovely. But what an early start!" said Mrs. Miliken from behind a pair of oversized sunglasses. She was clutching a coffee. "I'm going to see your mom in class this afternoon."

Danny stared at Mrs. Miliken for about fifteen seconds before he managed a nervous grin.

"Great," he said.

It seemed like forever until the light changed and the three rode off down the street.

"Why did you say the park?" asked Molly when they got to Pikesmith Street. "I thought you told your mother we were going swimming."

"All right, not a good start," Danny said. "I panicked."

The three followed a big green sign that pointed toward the Sunshine Parkway, and before long they were cruising up an on-ramp and onto the one-lane road.

It only took a few minutes before the city started to melt away, and within half an hour, the road dropped off into a green valley, then slowly began rising through the hills. Danny was struck by how much longer the hilly bits seemed when you were pedaling, and how you hardly noticed them at all when you were sitting in the back of your parents' car.

After nearly an hour of riding, Danny's brow was soaked with sweat. He glanced in a small mirror he had strapped to his left handlebar. Molly was gliding along, but Lucas had fallen a hundred yards behind and his face was as red as a hot dog. He was pedaling away furiously on his deliveryman's bike, but it didn't seem to be going anywhere.

Lucas was starting to get upset, cursing the bike, cursing the hill, and cursing Danny—and that was before the loud pop and the hollow clank.

The chain on Lucas's bike had come completely off its chainwheel. Lucas jumped off and was now literally hopping up and down in anger. They were an hour from home and two hours from West Bubble.

"Of all the stupid, pinhead, lame-o, dim-witted, backward, brain-dead ideas I've ever let you talk me into, this is the tops, Danny," Lucas ranted as Danny and Molly cycled back to him. "And I've been a part of some pretty stupid ideas since I met you."

"It's not Danny's fault," Molly objected. "You're the one riding a bike that should be in a museum!"

"Oh, excuse me, Miss My-Father-Buys-Me-Everything," shot back Lucas. "I'm so sorry that I don't have the latest state-of-the-art pedaling machine like you. I didn't know we were trying out for the Olympics."

"Keep that up and we can just leave you here, Doughboy," said Molly with a scowl. That quieted Lucas down pretty quickly.

"Do you think you can fix it, Molly?" Danny asked.

Molly was good with bicycles, and it was her tool kit.

"Oh, I can fix the bike," said Molly." But Lucas will still be a loser."

She punctuated this insult by putting her hand on her forehead and making her thumb and index finger into the letter L.

Lucas was glowering, but he realized he wasn't in a good position to make a comeback, so he just sulked as Molly turned the bike over and started working on the chain. It took about ten minutes for Molly and Danny to get the chain back on the chainwheel, pulling it on link by link.

By the time they were done, their hands were black with grease, and Danny's Sid Canova shirt had a large black handprint on it. Molly turned the bike back over and pushed it toward Lucas without saying a word, then rode off.

"What's eating her?" said Lucas as he got back on his bike.

"I think maybe what you said about her father," Danny said.

It took them another half hour to reach the exit for the Harry Tinkleford Highway.

Danny had known it was going to be big. But he hadn't factored in the cars and tractor-trailers whizzing by at sixty-five miles per hour in either direction. Or the choking exhaust fumes. Or the fact that the emergency lane had so many bumps and potholes that it made their teeth rattle and their behinds numb. It was like riding over a pile of bricks.

This time it was Molly who was not coping well. She flinched every time a car whooshed by, and her face was a mask of deep concentration as she tried to keep her bike straight. It was so light and the wheels were so narrow that it took every pothole badly.

"This is scary, Danny. What in the world were you thinking?" she yelled.

Lucas's face contorted into a scowl whenever he ran over a pothole or hit a bump, which was every ten seconds or so.

"Ouch! My butt is killing me," he screamed.

After five minutes, the ugly metal basket on Lucas's bike popped off. It looked as if the rest of the bike could fall apart at any second.

Danny frowned. The trip was quickly becoming the kind of colossal mistake that your friends make fun of you for, for the rest of your life. When Lucas's chain popped off again, eliciting curses from both Molly and Lucas, Danny realized there was no point in going on.

Danny got off his bike and threw it to the side of the road, smashing the rearview mirror. Typical, he thought. Bad luck.

He felt like a loser. He felt like a Sluggers fan.

"It's my fault," said Danny as Molly cycled up to him. Lucas was pushing his bike, the chain scraping along on the road.

"Darn right it is," said Lucas.

"I, ah, I'm sorry," said Danny. "I didn't think it would be this hard."

"Um-hmm," said Molly, rubbing her hands together. He'd never seen her look so stressed out.

"I owe you guys a big apology," he continued.

"The biggest!" Lucas huffed. "And you owe my butt a separate apology."

Danny laughed, and so did Molly. Lucas could be pretty funny, especially when he didn't mean to be.

Danny pulled the tuna-and-pineapple sandwiches

out of his backpack and passed them around. They were smushed from the tool kit rattling around inside his bag, and some of the bits of pineapple had pushed their way through the soggy white bread.

"Now, these, these are truly disgusting," said Molly after taking a bite. "Did you come up with this combo on your own? I think we can safely say you're never going to be a chef."

"Or a navigator!" said Lucas.

"Well, you guys can't say I never take you anyplace," Danny joked. He was feeling a little better, and he also figured the best way out of the endless ribbing that was coming to him was to just admit he had made a stupid mistake.

"I guess this is about the dumbest thing I ever thought of," Danny said.

Molly and Lucas just stood there without saying a word. It was hard to tell if they were still a little angry or just tired.

"So I guess we should head back home, huh?" Danny said, and was surprised when Molly and Lucas broke out of their trance and looked at him in disbelief.

"What are you talking about?" said Molly. "Home? You're not getting out of this that easily."

Lucas was even more resolved.

"I'm going to need surgery on my butt after today," he said, his face so close to Danny's that their noses almost touched. "I'm not going through that for nothing. We're going to get to that mansion if it's the last thing we do."

West Bubble

The town of West Bubble sat on the western tip of Ball Four Sound, just across the bay from East Bubble. There was no place in the middle called simply Bubble, which Danny thought was strange. The towns had been known as West Rock and East Rock before Manchester and Skidmore Boddlebrooks arrived and folks decided to change the names.

When Manchester Boddlebrooks moved to West Rock shortly after he came to America in 1881, he wasn't a bubble-gum tycoon yet, and he didn't weigh three hundred pounds. Some people say his name wasn't even Manchester back then, and he spoke English with a thick accent that nobody could place.

As his fortune and his waistline grew, Manchester's past became the stuff of newspaper speculation and high-society whispers. Some said he was born Barkos Benzoulous in a tiny Greek fishing village, and only got the idea to call himself Manchester when he saw the word written on the side of a ship. Others said he was of noble blood and a direct descendant of the great medieval king Charlemagne, who was also on the heavy side. One story had it that Manchester and Skidmore were orphaned by Ukrainian circus performers after a freak accident involving an elephant they thought they could teach to swing on the trapeze.

Whenever anyone asked Manchester directly, he would scratch his chin and pretend he couldn't remember.

"It was a long time ago," he would say. "Have a stick of gum."

Young Manchester's first job in West Rock was as a groundskeeper at the town park, where he saw his first game of baseball and quickly developed a love for the sport. In the evenings, he would go back to the small apartment he shared with Skidmore and work on his gum inventions. Back then, it was nearly impossible to blow a bubble with the chewing gum on the market — a sticky concoction called Tasty Tooth Wax made from the sap of a sapodilla tree. It was not a big hit. It tasted a bit like soggy cardboard.

Manchester knew he could make a better gum, and he would work late into the night, boiling down raspberries and peaches and other fruits for his recipes. Skidmore thought his brother was crazy, and the racket he produced in the kitchen each night made it impossible to sleep.

"What did we come to this country for? To make

fruit syrup in the middle of the night?" Skidmore would ask impatiently, usually at around three a.m. The only time Skidmore tried one of Manchester's concoctions his face broke out in puffy red blotches and he missed three days of work. It almost brought the brothers to blows.

But Manchester kept experimenting, and when he found a secret technique to make his gum more rubbery so that you could blow bubbles with it, he started selling the chewy treats at West Rock's only grocery store, E. L. Macau's Fine Foods. The gum cost a penny a pack, and it sold out in a single afternoon. The next day's batch was gone in an hour. By the third day a line snaked around the block. Mr. Macau was begging Manchester to make more.

And that's how it all started.

Within a month, Manchester was no longer cutting the grass at the West Rock park. He had hired a speech instructor to make him sound more American, a chef to prepare his prodigious meals, and a tailor to stitch together the gleaming white three-piece suits that would become his trademark. A year later, his company, Manchester Mastications, Inc., was churning out a million packs of gum a day, with a fleet of one thousand horsemen on hand to rush the new product far and wide.

By the time Manchester built his enormous mansion on the outskirts of what had become West Bubble, he was the most powerful person in town. The profits from Manchester Mastications had paid for everything from the town hall to the West Bubble Zoo. There were scholarships (and of course free gum) for the brightest West Bubble schoolchildren, and town fairs and a theater for the adults.

Above all, there were the parties.

In the 107 years following Manchester's sudden death, nobody in West Bubble had thrown a party that could hold a candle to his. The whole town would turn out for Manchester's parties, joined by the most famous entertainers, sportsmen, and politicians of the day. West Bubble filled to the brim with fancy horse-drawn carriages, each pulling up at the Boddlebrooks mansion laden with gifts for the host. Manchester always joined his guests at midnight, steering his enormous bubble-shaped hot-air balloon into the backyard as fireworks lit up the sky.

It wasn't long before West Bubble became the in place to be, and soon large mansions and fancy clubs sprang up all over town.

Everyone who was anyone moved to West Bubble.

Everyone except Skidmore Boddlebrooks.

Skidmore's jealousy grew with each new hit bubble-gum flavor his brother produced, and one day when he couldn't take it anymore, he packed his bags and moved across the bay to a large waterfront home in

East Bubble. Skidmore surrounded himself with new friends who all thought Manchester's gum was disgusting and his wacky mansion even worse. Rumor had it they didn't even like baseball.

In the evenings, Skidmore would stand on his porch and watch the fireworks and hear the raucous music wafting over the bay. Manchester always invited his brother to the festivities, but Skidmore never came.

Danny had learned all about the parties and the feud with Skidmore in Manchester Boddlebrooks's biography, *By Gum! The Boddle Behind the Bubble*, which he'd read three times.

But as he, Molly, and Lucas rode into West Bubble that morning, they saw little left over from the magical days described in the book. In the center of town, an eight-screen cineplex towered over the spot where Boddlebrooks's theater once stood. The old zoo had closed down too, and the facade of the pink granite town hall had turned black from pollution and neglect.

When they got to the town's main square, Danny stopped and pulled out the map, which had by now nearly disintegrated in his sweaty back pocket.

"I guess all we have to do is get down to the boardwalk over here," Danny said, pointing at a dotted line on the map at the edge of the water. "Then we just hop over to Winning-Streak Watermelon Road and we're almost home."

Molly and Lucas were too tired to do more than grunt.

Danny guided his friends toward the beach. The wide streets were lined with the enormous homes of the past century's rich and famous, but they all seemed to have lost the battle against wind and salt and sand.

The whole place needed a paint job, Danny thought, though the truth was that he, Molly, and Lucas weren't in much better shape.

Danny and Molly were covered in grease from fixing Lucas's bicycle chain nine times, and Molly's long red hair had had a particularly bad reaction to the wind and stress of the highway. She looked as if she'd gotten it stuck in a vacuum cleaner.

The speedometer had fallen off Lucas's bike, and some of the seat stuffing had torn away. Lucas had worked out a way to cycle standing up that spared his behind further bruising, but it meant jerking his bike back and forth underneath him like a joystick and it seemed to require an excessive amount of grunting and grimacing.

The trio got more than a few stares from the West Bubblians who crossed their path, but they didn't care. It was a beautiful summer day, with blue skies and a slight breeze, and they were not at Quincy Park or at the pool or hanging out at someone's apartment.

They were in West Bubble, the farthest any of them had gotten from home on their own power, and they were about to see the Boddlebrooks mansion.

"Danny, I have to hand it to you. My entire body hurts, but this is great!" said Lucas as they pulled onto the boardwalk, their wheels clanking up and down against the wooden planks. Molly was beaming too, taking in the sea air and smiling at the curious towns-people.

At the end of the boardwalk, the three found Winning-Streak Watermelon Road, like the bubble gum, named optimistically by Boddlebrooks himself just before the Sluggers' inaugural year.

They were almost there. According to the map, the Boddlebrooks mansion was about a half mile outside town.

Danny took a deep breath and held it for twenty seconds for good luck, a trick he used whenever a pinch hitter came in with a runner on third base and less than two outs.

Danny's heart was racing and he started pedaling faster and faster. Molly must have been even more excited because she was fifty yards ahead and the gap was growing all the time.

As Danny rounded a bend in the road, he saw

Molly pointing to a big wooden sign. Most of the paint had flaked off, and what was left was nearly the same gray color as the weather-beaten signboard, but the words still jumped out:

BODDLEBROOKS MANSION
ALL SLUGGERS FANS WELCOME

The sign pointed across the road, to an enormous iron gate that once had been painted watermelon red. The top of the gate arched into a swirling peak where the letters M.B. stood proudly.

Lucas tapped the gate with his front tire and it slowly creaked open, wobbling on its rusty hinges. He looked at Danny and Molly and smiled.

"I'd never believe it if I didn't see it with my own eyes," he said. "We made it!"

Leading away from the gate through high fields of corn was a long gravel drive, flanked by tall privet hedges. The hedges had not been cut in a while, and they had begun to bend inward, so much so that they seemed to be falling in on each other. It gave Danny the feeling he was riding through a tunnel.

He tried to peer around the corners of the winding drive, but the hedges were too tall to see over and too thick to see through.

Danny thought of all the Sluggers fans that must

have come down this path. Men like his grandfather and great-grandfather, and boys and girls long since grown who filled a century of stadium seats and suffered a century of sorrows.

Boddlebrooks himself had made his final journey along this drive, followed by thousands of mourners for the tycoon-sized funeral.

Danny read that even President McKinley had come to the mansion for the ceremony. The country came to a standstill for a whole minute on that sad fall day; the only sound from coast to coast was the snap of tens of millions of bubbles blown in solidarity.

Danny, Molly, and Lucas rode on in silence, but the drive seemed to twist and turn endlessly ahead of them.

It felt like an eternity. Danny was just beginning to wonder if they would ever reach the house when the driveway opened like the mouth of a river and the canopy of hedges disappeared from above their heads.

And there it was.

The Boddlebrooks Mansion

"Gosh!" said Lucas.

"Wow!" said Molly.

Danny said nothing. He was speechless.

Standing in front of them, across an overgrown,

diamond-shaped lawn, was the most extraordinary building Danny had ever seen. It had four giant turrets, just like a castle, but each one was the shape of a baseball bat soaring into the sky. There were dozens of round windows at the top of the building, each with curved red windowpanes imitating a baseball's stitched double seam. In the center of the mansion was what had to be the most unusual front door ever made, thirty feet high and shaped like two oversized hot dogs standing back to back.

And of course, the building was red.

Not just any red, but the most mind-boggling red the three friends had ever seen. The mansion looked like a giant piece of bubble gum that you could pop right into your mouth—if you had the biggest mouth in the world, that is.

As they rode closer, it became clear that the house was falling apart. The right side had sunk into the ground, making it look as if it were about to slide away from the rest of the mansion, and one of the baseball-bat towers had a long crack that ran down the middle.

It didn't matter to Danny. He thought the place was magnificent.

Molly led the way down a gravel path along the edge of the diamond-shaped lawn to the front door. It was by far the biggest door Danny had ever seen, and certainly the only one shaped like two hot dogs. Danny wished he'd brought a camera so he could show Willie the Hot Dog Man.

"This place is amazing!" Lucas whispered as he stared up at the building.

There were two iron knockers, one on either side of the door, each shaped like an *S* as in Sluggers, and each about the size of Danny's head. Molly grabbed hold of one and started knocking. Nobody stirred.

"Hello, is anybody home?" Lucas yelled, but still nobody came.

Soon all three of them were banging on the door with all their might, shouting for someone to come and let them in. The banging echoed through the mansion.

"What if nobody is around?" asked Molly after a few minutes. "What if they've already closed the place down?"

That was a possibility Danny had never even contemplated.

"There must be another way in," he said.

Danny led the others around the side of the great house. There had to be another door or a bell to ring or something.

He stood on tiptoe and peaked in the high windows, but the curtains were drawn and it didn't look as though there were any lights on inside. Danny tried tapping a windowpane with his finger.

"Hello! Hello! Anybody home?" he yelled. But there was not even a hint of movement behind the drapes.

They walked on, peering in all the windows and taking turns shouting out as they went.

"Do you think the hot-air balloon is still on the back lawn?" asked Lucas. "I wonder if the fountain still spouts bubble-gum-flavored soda. Do you think you can just scoop it out and drink it?"

"I bet it would be flat by now," Molly said.

When they turned the corner to the back of the building, it was clear that there had been no hot-air balloon landings and no bubble-gum parties for some time.

The grass hadn't been cut in years. There were tracks of hedgerows planted in a mazelike pattern, but they were all dead. Cracked red marble steps swept down from the back of the mansion, separating the garden into three descending tiers, each one more overgrown than the next, until they fell off into the sea.

The famous fountain was there, but it was bone dry and cracked. The only sign that it had ever spouted anything at all was a thin pink ring where the water level used to be.

The place looked more like an abandoned lot than a bubble-gum tycoon's backyard, but it was still grand in a sad, forgotten sort of way. It was like finding an archaeological site with the ruins of an ancient civilization, Danny thought.

But what use was it if they couldn't get in?

"Hey, look at that," Molly said. She pointed up to one of the tall rectangular windows that ran along the back of the house, about six feet off the ground.

"Yeah, it's a window," Lucas snorted. "There are a million of them."

"Yes, but this one is open," she said.

And she was right. Along the bottom of the window was a thin, dark crack.

"Okay, that's our ticket in," Lucas said. "Molly, if Danny and I give you a boost, do you think you could push the window up a foot or two?"

"Yeah, I think so," Molly said before catching herself. "But isn't this, like, illegal?"

Lucas looked exasperated.

"You're such a Goody Two-Shoes," he said, lacing his hands together with Danny's to make a human step stool.

"We're not going to take anything," Lucas continued. "We're just going to have a look around. Don't you think we deserve a look around?"

Molly shrugged.

"I've got to get some more normal friends," she said, but she clambered up on their hands anyway.

Molly pushed up on the window with both arms and Danny strained to keep his hands in place. The window inched up a fraction.

She pushed again. Nothing.

"It's like trying to lift a car," Molly sputtered, her face about as red as the mansion. Lucas and Danny were grimacing too.

"Give it some muscle," Lucas said.

"I'm trying," Molly shouted back.

"What are you kids doing?" a voice hissed from behind them.

Danny was horrified to see a shadow creeping up the wall.

Molly shrieked and Lucas and Danny both staggered back, leaving her hanging from the window ledge, her feet dangling about a foot off the ground.

Danny and Lucas turned slowly, and when they did, they found themselves face to face with the oldest, most wrinkled man they'd ever seen. He was bent over a rounded wooden cane and had patches of white whiskers sprouting out of his face. He must have been tall once, but now he was so stooped he had to tilt his head up to talk to them.

"You there, how did you get back here? What are you doing with my window?" the man continued, one of his milky eyes fixed firmly on Danny, the other wandering frighteningly off to the right. "There are no visitors allowed back here without me."

Danny tried to speak but nothing came out. He couldn't stop staring at the old man's scary wobbling eyes. Lucas was doing little better, managing a few squeaking sounds.

Molly had lowered herself from the window ledge and was the first one to actually formulate a word.

"Uh," she said nervously.

It was something, at least.

"We, ah . . . Well, sir, we didn't mean any harm," she went on. Danny and Lucas were staring at her in silent admiration, one nodding in agreement and the other shaking his head no. "We didn't think anyone was here. We knocked on the front door."

One of the old man's eyes was focused on the open window, while the other scanned the terrified faces.

"Well, I'm here. I'm always here! And you can't just go marching around willy-nilly wherever you choose," he snapped.

"No, sir," said Molly. "We were just leaving, actually."

But the old man didn't seem to hear her.

"Anyway, I imagine you've come to look at the mansion," he said, his voice softening into a hoarse croak. "I guess there's no harm in that. We don't get too many visitors these days."

Molly looked at Lucas and Lucas looked at Danny. Danny shrugged and raised his eyebrows.

"Come with me," said the old man. "The tour starts at the front."

Old Man in an Old House

The man walked briskly for someone his age. In fact, it occurred to Danny that he had never seen anyone that ancient walking at all.

The old man led the group back around to the front door. He put his cane aside and reached into the pocket of his baggy pants, one eye cast downward and the other looking straight ahead at the giant keyhole. After fumbling around for a minute, he pulled out a long iron skeleton key, the kind Danny thought pirates might use to open treasure chests.

He turned the key with a hollow clank and the heavy wooden door creaked open. Danny felt a rush of cold air across the threshold as he followed the old man inside, and Lucas and Molly pushed in behind them.

They found themselves in a cavernous hallway, as grand as you would expect any room behind a thirty-foot-tall door to be. The ceiling was so high Danny wondered if he would be able to hit it if he threw a ball into the air. The base of the walls was made of intricately carved mahogany panels. Higher up, the panels gave way to a deep ruby red wallpaper, covered almost entirely by old photographs and oil paintings, including a life-sized painting of a young Manchester Boddlebrooks standing next to a horse.

On either side, a marble staircase swept up to the second floor, and tucked beneath them was a wide double door.

The old man put the key back in his pocket, turned around, and set his gaze on the three children in front of him, who were standing so close together in the middle of the room they were practically on each other's feet.

"The name is Seymour Sycamore," he wheezed, leaning on his cane. "And I've been takin' care of the Boddlebrooks home for decades.

"I know every inch of these grounds," he said. "The house comprises 127 rooms in all and it sleeps 118 adults and 34 children comfortably. It takes 1,500 lightbulbs to light the place. There are seven miles of carpets, and if you stripped off all the wallpaper and laid it end to end, it would stretch from here to Paris, France."

Mr. Sycamore looked Danny, Molly, and Lucas in the eyes for emphasis before he went on.

"There's the ballroom, a billiard room, a popcorn room, the kitchen. And then of course the bedrooms. Fifty-two of them in all, you know? Now, what would you like to see first?"

"We wouldn't want to trouble you," Danny said. "We could just show ourselves around."

"Nonsense!" hissed Mr. Sycamore, swiveling his head up to look at Danny. "Nobody shows themselves around.

"And besides," he said sadly. "We haven't had any visitors since they closed the place for renovations a number of years back. This may be my last chance to do this. They're tearing the place down, did you hear? People have no respect for history these days!"

"That's why we're here!" Danny shouted, gaining a bit of confidence. "We want to save the mansion."

"Oh, young fella, I'm afraid that's impossible," the old man said, one eye on Danny and the other twinkling up at the Boddlebrooks painting on the wall above his head. "They've signed all the paperwork. It's just a matter of time. Why, this mansion and me, we're both on our last legs. Anyway, I'll show you around the place while there's still a place to show."

Mr. Sycamore led them through the double door under the stairs and down a short hallway to the next room. He threw open the doors with a flourish, and Danny had to pinch himself to make sure he wasn't dreaming.

The room was even bigger than the one they'd come from, with dark walls and a glittering chandelier that was about the size of Danny's bedroom at home. All around the room was a wooden walkway, which they were standing on, and in the middle was a brass popcorn machine about the size of a car.

Millions upon millions of fluffy popcorn kernels littered the floor, an ocean of popcorn that came right up to Danny's chest. Danny glanced up at four copper chutes that came down from the walls above their heads and stretched into the center of the room.

"That's where the butter comes out," explained Mr. Sycamore.

"Wow!" said Lucas.

Danny reached out and grabbed some popcorn and stuck it in his mouth. He realized immediately that it was a bad idea.

"Blech!" Danny croaked, looking unsuccessfully for a place to spit it out. It was vile, like eating moldy chalk.

"Well, what do you expect?" said Mr. Sycamore. "Why, that popcorn must be more than a hundred years old. This room was left exactly as it was when the great man died. All the rooms are like that."

Molly put her finger in her mouth and made a vomiting face at Danny.

"One-hundred-year-old popcorn," she laughed. "Now that's gross."

She turned to Mr. Sycamore.

"I wouldn't have thought popcorn could last that long," she said.

"Well, young lady, you're right," he said. "We had a science professor in here one time and he said he reckoned it was on account of the cold temperature in the house that keeps things fresh longer. I just think there's something about this place that keeps things alive. Just look at me!"

In any case, Danny thought, it had been a bad day for food. The pineapple and tuna were already at war inside Danny's stomach, and the hundred-year-old popcorn was sure to add to it.

"Now, there are dozens of rooms on the ground level, and each one is unique," Mr. Sycamore said. "I'll show you all of them, but first I must tell you the house rules.

"It is very, very important that you obey the rules," Mr. Sycamore said, lowering his voice and pointing with his cane for emphasis.

"Yes, sir," Molly, Danny, and Lucas answered in unison.

Mr. Sycamore was a lot less frightening in the mansion than he had been when he snuck up on them, but there was still something unnerving about him, especially when his wandering eye narrowed to a glare and fixed on a spot just above your head.

"Firstly, you are not to touch anything," Mr. Sycamore said. "Secondly, you are not to wander around by yourselves. I must be with you at all times.

"Thirdly . . ." Mr. Sycamore's voice trailed off. "Now what was thirdly?"

The eye looked up at the ceiling.

"Oh, yes. Thirdly . . . you are not to eat any of the popcorn! Is that quite clear?" Mr. Sycamore said.

"Very clear," said Danny, and the others nodded.

They moved on to the cotton-candy room, which had wisps of pink cotton candy hanging from all the walls and a sticky cotton-candy carpet on the floor. Danny had learned his lesson and didn't eat any.

Then it was time for the kitchen. There were fifteen wood-burning stoves and a long table about the length of a bowling lane to chop things on. All along the walls hung pots and pans, some so big you could climb inside them. There were brass spoons the size of pogo sticks and an old-fashioned bread-toasting machine that took fifty slices at a time.

"Mr. Boddlebrooks had a very large appetite," Mr. Sycamore explained.

In his day, Manchester employed thirty chefs, and thirty more were brought in on party nights, Mr. Sycamore said. Manchester had also devised a series of bells with different sounds, so he could order his favorite foods from anywhere in the house. One bell that made a deep resonating sound meant he wanted breakfast cereal. A smaller one that made a high-pitched tinkle meant beef jerky. An order from Manchester would send the cooking staff scurrying, and it wouldn't be long before the snack was brought to him.

Mr. Sycamore was right. Each room did have something special about it.

The billiard balls in the billiard room were painted to look like baseballs instead of having stripes and spots as on a normal table. The laundry room was big enough to service an army, and there were still a couple of old Sluggers jerseys hanging out on a line.

"We left them there out of respect," Mr. Sycamore said.

The ballroom was so big you could have played a baseball game inside it. Twenty-four chandeliers hung down on long chains from the ceiling, which was covered by millions of tiny mirrors.

As they walked down a long hallway that led away from the ballroom, Danny noticed a tall wooden door with the inscription M.B. on it in flowing letters. Just as his fingers grasped the brass doorknob, Danny heard the loud crack of Mr. Sycamore's cane.

"Stop . . . right . . . there," said the old man, his eyes bouncing around like pinballs. "That room is not part of the tour."

Danny's hand sprang off the knob immediately.

"Now please follow me upstairs," Mr. Sycamore continued, recovering his composure. "We have fifty-two bedrooms to see, and I don't want you getting into any more mischief."

"Yes, sir," Danny said, but he didn't think it was fair.

"What's in there, Mr. Sycamore?" Lucas asked.

"It is off-limits," said the old man. "It used to be Mr. Boddlebrooks's personal study. He never allowed anyone in there while he was alive. Before he died, Mr. Boddlebrooks wrote a will, and in it he forbade anyone to go in there once he was dead too. You might say he felt kind of strongly about it.

"As long as I'm in charge here, nobody ever will go in that study!" Mr. Sycamore said.

The old man led the way back to the main hallway and up the marble staircase to the second floor. It took quite an effort for Mr. Sycamore to climb the stairs, and when he got to the top he was breathing heavily. Danny thought he was going to keel over.

"As I have said," Mr. Sycamore croaked between gulps of air, "Mr. Boddlebrooks had fifty-two bedrooms, each one dedicated to a different one of his delicious gum flavors.

"I will take you into a few of the bedrooms now," he went on, leaning one hand on his cane and another against a wall. Even his wandering eye looked tired.

"Are you sure you're okay, Mr. Sycamore?" Molly asked. "We could just, you know, look around while you sit down somewhere."

"No, no, no! I've done this a million times. I'm fine," Mr. Sycamore insisted.

They were standing in a long hallway, and on either side of it were a series of doors. Above each door was a number, and each one had a plaque with a bubble-gum flavor written in fancy lettering.

Mr. Sycamore took the group over to door number one, "Classic Bubble Gum." Across the way was door number two, "Spearmint Strikeout." Just down the hall they could make out number three, "Grand-Slam Grape," and number four, "Tutti-Frutti Triple."

Mr. Sycamore turned the knob to door number one and they all piled in. The walls and ceiling were painted pink, and the floor had a pink carpet. Even the bedsheets on the old-fashioned four-poster bed were pink, and the bed had the words CLASSIC BUBBLE GUM carved into the headboard. It was like being inside a pink bubble.

On the desk they found dozens of century-old boxes of Classic Bubble Gum. A drawing on the boxes showed a serious-looking man in a fancy suit standing next to a smiling woman in a big puffy dress. Both were blowing bubbles, and underneath them the caption read: "Boddlebrooks Classic Bubble Gum, delicious fun for gentlemen and ladies alike."

They looked in the bathroom, which had pink marble walls with a big pink tub. There was a baseball-shaped stained-glass window above the bath.

"Did Manchester sleep in this room?" Lucas asked Mr. Sycamore, who was sitting on the bed catching his breath.

"Sometimes," he said. "Mr. Boddlebrooks slept in a different room every week, and after a full year— fifty-two weeks—he would start over again."

"Why'd he do that?" asked Molly. "It seems like an awful lot of bother moving all your things around each week."

Mr. Sycamore looked at her strangely.

"Mr. Boddlebrooks never moved his own things from room to room," he said. "That was a job for the staff, and they were honored to do it."

"Sure," said Molly. "It's just a little . . . eccentric, don't you think?"

"Not at all," Mr. Sycamore snapped. "What would you do if you had fifty-two bubble-gum bedrooms? Just let fifty-one of them go to waste? Now that would be eccentric."

It was hard to argue with Mr. Sycamore's logic.

"Come along! Come along!" the old man said. "We mustn't dawdle!"

As they made their way through the upstairs halls, the flavors got stranger and stranger, and so did the rooms.

Number seventeen was "Simply Sauerkraut," and it had cabbage-colored wallpaper and stringy beige drapes. It smelled a bit like Willie the Hot Dog Man's cart.

Number thirty-two was "Patently Peanut Shell." The floor was an inch deep with pulverized peanuts, and in one corner was a grinding machine half filled with roasted nuts. Even the bed was peanut-shaped.

Room number forty-seven was "Rosin-Bag Raspberry." That didn't sound so tasty.

Each of the rooms was different, some with big wooden beds and wide chests of drawers, some with rocking chairs and tall bookshelves filled with dusty old books. Each had a box of gum on the desk, but most of the boxes looked empty.

They dashed inside so many rooms Danny's head began to spin. He couldn't imagine what it must have been like to be Boddlebrooks, moving from room to room every week, throwing his fantastic parties.

The last room, number fifty-two, was "Bench-warmer Banana," which was ringed by the same thick wooden bench you'd see in the Sluggers' dugout.

"Well, that's the end of the tour," Mr. Sycamore said, plopping down on the bench and leaning his cane against the wall. "I hope you've enjoyed it and I'm sorry I couldn't let you go in the study. House rules, you know."

Danny, Molly, and Lucas each took a seat on the bench. They might not have been as old as Mr. Sycamore, but they had had a pretty long day too.

"You're one strong old dude, Mr. Sycamore," Lucas said. "My grandfather would never have been able to go through all those rooms. Heck, even I'm tired. How do you do it?"

But Mr. Sycamore didn't answer. He was fast asleep, slumped over his cane and snoring softly, one eye shut but the other still moving about on its own.

Lucas bent down and snapped his fingers in front of Mr. Sycamore's open eye, but the old man didn't stir.

"Now that is strange," Lucas said.

"Should we wake him up?" asked Molly. "We really need to be getting home. It's already two o'clock."

"Nah, let's let him rest a bit," said Danny. "I want to see that last room."

"What last room?" said Molly.

"You know, the study," Danny said.

"Oh no you don't!" Molly whispered. "There's no way we are going in there! Didn't you see how angry he got when you just touched the knob?"

Even Lucas looked unsure, and Danny had never seen Lucas shy away from potential trouble.

"The thing is, Danny, his eye is still open!" Lucas said under his breath, glancing at Mr. Sycamore warily. "I mean, maybe he can still see us even if he is asleep. Maybe it's some sort of a trap."

"Besides, Danny, we've got to head back soon or we'll never get home in time. My mother will go crazy, and once she starts calling around and finds out we lied, we're all dead," Molly said.

Danny had stopped listening, though. He put his hands on his knees and took a long, hard look at Mr. Sycamore's face. Other than the eye, which was dancing about the room as if it had lost something important, he seemed to be sleeping like a baby.

"Just give me five minutes," Danny said, backing away quietly.

Lucas nodded and Molly rolled her eyes.

"You guys stay here and keep him busy if he does

wake up," Danny said. "Don't worry. Nothing can possibly go wrong."

The Study

Danny tiptoed out of the room and down the long hallway. He crept quietly down the stairs and through the corridor to the study.

Danny turned the knob and the door opened smoothly.

Behind it was a narrow room with Persian rugs on the floor and tall bookshelves lining every wall, each filled with hundreds of leather-bound books. Heavy red velvet curtains hung down from two tall windows opposite the study door, and between them was a grandfather clock. The curtains were open a crack in the center, allowing just enough sunlight for Danny to be able to look around.

At the far end of the room sat a massive wooden desk covered in yellowing papers, and an extra-wide leather chair. Behind that, between a pair of bookshelves, was a wide closet built into the wall.

Danny took a seat in the chair (Boddlebrooks's chair!) and looked up at the ceiling. It was too beautiful for words.

The center held a round panel with a vivid oil painting of the Boddlebrooks mansion. There were twelve panels around it, each painted to depict a separate story from the Sluggers' first season.

Danny glanced from panel to panel. The first one was of smiling Sluggers players limbering up during spring training; then there was one of a packed Winning Streak Stadium on opening day; then one of all the ballplayers huddled around in the clubhouse, with legendary manager Luke Slocum delivering a speech.

The panels went right up though the play-offs, but the final one, which Danny guessed should have been of the celebration of the Sluggers' first and only championship, was blank. Boddlebrooks must never have had the chance to have it completed, Danny thought.

He got up and opened the closet door. Hanging inside were several wooden bats, their handles black with pine tar, and an extra-extra-extra-large Sluggers uniform with the name Boddlebrooks stitched on the back. The great man's own uniform! It was like heaven.

Danny closed the door and walked around the room, scanning the bookshelves. Each wall was dedicated to a different subject. One held books about baseball, another was almost exclusively about bubble gum, and another was filled only with history books. There was a shelf with several volumes about

74

the town of West Bubble and another, interestingly, that included a five-part history of circus acts.

Danny was about to sneak back upstairs to find Molly and Lucas when he heard a sound that made the hair on the back of his neck stand on end.

Clomp! Clomp! Clomp!

It was the unmistakable thump of Mr. Sycamore's cane coming along the corridor.

"When I find that little rascal . . . ," Mr. Sycamore's voice boomed.

Danny froze.

"Oh no, Mr. Sycamore, I'm sure he's not in the study," Danny heard Lucas say. "He must have gone to the bathroom."

"We'll just see about that," the old man said, and Danny realized the voice was coming from right outside the door.

His heart was racing, and he looked around desperately for a place to hide.

Danny lunged for the closet and scrambled inside, pulling the door closed behind him just as the study door creaked open.

"You children wait out in the hall," he heard Mr. Sycamore snap. "Nobody is allowed in here but me."

Danny could feel his heart pounding in the darkness. It was remarkably cold and musty in the closet, and there was a strange fruity smell that he couldn't identify. Through the keyhole, Danny could see Mr. Sycamore shuffling around the study, poking back the curtains with his cane.

"Are you in here, son?" Mr. Sycamore called out. "You better come out this instant if you are."

As the old man drew closer, Danny held his breath and counted backward from eleven for good luck.

Mr. Sycamore was just on the other side of the closet door, so close that it sounded as if he were wheezing right into Danny's ear.

As the stooped figure brushed by the door, Danny found to his horror that he was staring straight into one of the old man's eyes, which was right on the other side of the keyhole.

He prayed it was the one that didn't work.

"All right, mister," the old man said. "I guess you aren't in here after all."

The eyeball pulled away from the keyhole, and soon Danny could hear the fall of Mr. Sycamore's cane pulling farther away. The study door opened and closed with a click, and silence again filled the room.

Danny let out a deep breath. Why hadn't Mr. Sycamore opened the closet door? Just lucky, Danny thought. He leaned back in relief, but instead of a wall, his shoulders met thin air. Danny stumbled backward in surprise.

He put his hand out behind him and felt for the

back of the closet, but there was nothing there. Just darkness.

He turned and took a few steps deeper into the closet, waving his hands before him so as not to bump into anything. Nothing.

After a few more paces, Danny began to realize he was not in a closet at all, but instead in some sort of passageway. He moved haltingly, deeper and deeper into the darkness, until finally he hit something wooden. It was another door!

Danny grabbed the knob, swung the door open, and gasped.

The Round Room

Danny was standing in a round stone room with impossibly high walls. There was a small circular window about fifteen feet above his head through which the sun cast a sharp beam of light on a long wooden table and chair in the center of the room.

The walls were lined with curved wooden shelves stacked with broken glass beakers and jars, just like the ones they used in science class in school.

Danny stood up straight and brushed himself off. Where could he be? He craned his neck to look at the ceiling, but it was so high above him he could barely make it out. It was like being inside a chimney or a tower, he thought.

That was it! He must be inside one of the baseball-bat towers that stood at each corner of the house!

On the table were piles of experimenting equipment: silver mixing spoons, brass funnels, round glass petri dishes, and a glass measuring jar. There were several old books on the table, each as big as a dictionary. Some were written in a foreign language Danny couldn't recognize. Others, written in English, had the strangest titles: *Fruit and Karma: A Digestive Guide to the Stars*, *The Power of Sour*, and *Infusion Solutions: It Boils Down to Fortune*.

Danny lifted up one of the heavy books and his eye lit on a small tin box that had been partially hidden alongside it.

It was about the size of a cigar box, and it was covered in dust.

Danny bent down and blew as hard as he could. The dust rushed up off the box and billowed back into his face. When he opened his eyes, he could see the picture of a baseball player with knee-length pants and a funny little cap looking toward the sky. Across the top of the box, the word TESTING was written in red letters.

Underneath the baseball player, handwritten in the same fancy script as on the study door, it said:

LONGEST-LASTING   KOSMIC   KRANBERRY — MANCHESTER

E. BODDLEBROOKS'S 53RD EXCITING FLAVOR.

Danny's hands were shaking. A fifty-third flavor? Everyone knew Boddlebrooks had only made fifty-two kinds of gum.

He lifted the lid, and to his surprise, the box was filled with gum, packets and packets of the stuff, all good as new. Each packet had a cranberry-colored wrapper dotted with tiny constellations of silver stars — Orion's Belt, the Big Dipper, and even one that looked remarkably like a large bubble-gum tycoon.

Could this have been what Boddlebrooks was working on when he died? Danny wondered. He rifled through the box and started to carefully peel back one of the wrappers.

Bong! . . . Bong! . . . Bong!

Danny heard the faint chime of the grandfather clock in the study striking three. He remembered his friends, and Mr. Sycamore's angry eyeball. Now it really was time to go. They'd never get back to the city in time.

He quickly snatched three packets of gum and stuck them deep in his pocket, then raced through the dark-ened corridor to the closet door.

He took a quick peek through the keyhole to make sure the coast was clear, then crept out of the closet and slipped through the study door.

As he ran to join his friends, Danny tapped his fin-gers against the gum in his pocket.

THIRD  INNING

The Return

Danny turned the key to the front door of his family's apartment at 6:23 p.m., nearly two and a half hours later than he had told his mother he would be home.

To be half an hour late was almost expected; an hour was cause for minor scolding. But Danny knew that his parents' panic buttons would have gone off at the ninety-minute mark. Phone calls would have been made to the Masterlys and Molly's mom. Cover stories would have unraveled.

In short, it would be all-out parental pandemonium.

Danny figured his mother and father would be somewhere between worried stiff and purple-faced with fire-breathing fury. He only hoped their anger would be tempered by the relief of seeing their little angel home safe and sound.

He was wrong.

"Daniel Gurkin! Is that you?" boomed his father's voice from the living room, even before the front door had thudded shut behind him. "Where have you been?!"

That was a bad sign. His father normally didn't get back from the campaign until after dark, even on weekends. Danny could hear his mother's voice all the way from the living room. That was an even worse sign.

"Get him in here, Harold," Lydia Gurkin said. "I want to see that boy."

Danny gulped. He tried to remember one of the cover stories he, Molly, and Lucas had thought up on the long bike ride home. Lucas suggested they pretend they had been trapped under a fallen tree in Quincy Park or had lost their short-term memories after being knocked on the head by a steel beam.

Molly had come up with a slightly better story involving a heroic effort to rescue a cat that had fallen down a manhole, but it still seemed a bit far-fetched: how to explain the grease-covered clothes, the wind-frazzled hair, the heap of metal that was now Lucas's bike?

Mr. and Mrs. Gurkin were sitting side by side on the

living room couch, and Max was reclining in his favorite position in the easy chair across from them, silver earphones jutting out of each ear and a blank look on his face.

Danny looked at his father. He was definitely above a seven on the Fatherly Rage Richter scale.

"We've been scouring the neighborhood for you. Look at your poor mother! We were five minutes away from calling the police," Harold Gurkin said, jabbing a finger at his watch.

Danny stared at the floor. He had to come up with something to say, and quickly. He considered Lucas's amnesia defense.

"Well, ah . . . you see, the thing is," Danny said. His throat was dry.

"You have exactly one minute to explain yourself, young man," Harold Gurkin said, rising to his feet and glaring down at Danny.

"Dad . . . Mom . . . I have a confession to make," Danny began slowly. "I . . . ah . . . I didn't actually go swimming with Molly and Lucas today."

"I don't want to know where you weren't! I want to know where you were!" Harold Gurkin shouted. "I've had Molly's mother and Mr. Masterly on the phone already. I've rung the pool. They haven't seen any of you kids all day, so where were you?"

"Daniel . . . ," Lydia Gurkin said. "I want some

answers. No excuses. No tall tales. Answers!"

Danny looked from his father to his mother and then back down at his sneakers.

Less than half an hour before, he, Molly, and Lucas had pulled over on the corner of Pikesmith Street and taken a solemn oath never to admit, even under intense interrogation, to having left the city limits.

Wild horses would not drag a confession out of them!

"We never would have done it if you'd had time for us!" Danny shouted. "I asked you to take us! I asked Mom! We asked Lucas's parents and Molly's father. Nobody would do it, so we had no choice!"

There was an excruciating silence, like the pause just before a roller coaster plunges down the steepest of drops.

"Danny Gurkin, did you . . . ? You didn't! Are you trying to tell me that you somehow went to the Boddlebrooks mansion? You kids went to West Bubble?" his father said in disbelief. "You didn't. . . . You would-n't!"

"We did!" Danny said defiantly, stomping his foot. "We wanted to save the mansion and nobody would help us!"

"Did Lucas Masterly put you up to this?" Lydia Gurkin said.

"No," Danny admitted. "It was my idea."

"You took a bus to West Bubble?" Harold Gurkin shouted.

"Not exactly," Danny replied.

Mr. Gurkin thought for a minute.

"You got the train?"

"Not exactly."

There was a pause.

"You couldn't have . . . ah, I mean, you wouldn't possibly have— You kids didn't bike all the way out to West Bubble, did you?" his father shouted.

"Yes. That's just what we did," Danny replied.

"You took your bikes on the highway?" his mother asked.

"Well, just a bit," Danny replied.

"Oh . . . my . . . God!" she said, shaking her head slowly from side to side.

"I want you to go to your room and think about what you have done," Mr. Gurkin said. "Your mother and I will decide what kind of punishment is appropriate."

"How about hanging," came a voice from the easy chair.

"Max!" snapped Mrs. Gurkin.

Danny shuffled back to his room and flopped on the bed.

That really hadn't gone well at all.

The Disappearance of Lou Smegny

On the night Manchester Boddlebrooks died, tumbling over like a giant walrus onto poor Lou Smegny, a young newspaper reporter standing in the clubhouse swore he heard the bubble-gum tycoon whisper three final words in the smothered shortstop's ear.

It was hard to make out what they were amid the gasps and screams of the clubhouse, even harder since Manchester's mouth was full of pretzel dough, but it sounded distinctly as if he whispered: "Chew it, Lou."

A few Sluggers players who witnessed the episode said they saw Lou Smegny nod and mumble something back just before he lost consciousness under the enormous weight of the dead man.

But police investigators concluded that no conversation ever took place. They said Boddlebrooks was likely already dead before he hit the ground and certainly wouldn't have been able to formulate words with a chunk of pretzel caught in his throat. Plus, why would anybody say "Chew it, Lou" before he died?

It took a crew of ten men to lift the fallen bubble-gum tycoon off Smegny, who was then dragged out of the clubhouse and rushed to the hospital in a horse-drawn ambulance.

Smegny lay unconscious in the hospital for a week, his back broken and his body shattered. By the time he woke up, the reporter who had heard Boddlebrooks's final words had been reassigned to another story, and nobody was around to ask the injured shortstop what they had meant.

Not long after that, Smegny himself disappeared, checking out of the hospital on a stormy November night and limping onto a train heading north to Canada.

The nurse on duty on Lou Smegny's last night said the young ballplayer was so stooped over he could barely walk. He didn't look up once as he filled out the paperwork for his discharge. She pleaded with him to get back into bed, but he was a grown man and she could only watch as he hobbled out the front door.

For several years, the Sluggers tried to track down the unfortunate shortstop for old-timers' games and opening-day reunions. They took out newspaper ads and hired private investigators. But there was no record of him anywhere.

The club decided to dedicate one game a year to Smegny, hoping it might prompt him to show up again one day.

He never did, but to this day on Smegny Night, the Sluggers hand out seat-cushion dolls that look just like him. As they take their seats on top of the cushions, fans are told to think back on the fateful night when a much larger man fell over and crushed the real thing.

For most people, that was the end of Lou Smegny, but in fact, there was one final sighting of the shortstop. A group of Sluggers fans traveling to a hair-tonic convention in Canada on the night Smegny checked out of the hospital reported seeing the hobbled ballplayer sitting by himself in a darkened carriage on a northbound train.

"Hey, Lou," one of the men shouted when he realized who it was. "Tough break, kid. But you'll get well again. You'll win another championship for the big bubble-gum tycoon in the sky."

But Smegny didn't seem to hear the man, and he didn't look up when the gentleman tried to sell him a bottle of Extra-Potent Rhubarb Hair Tonic.

The shortstop just slouched in his seat and stared out the window, his eyes dancing in their sockets like pinballs.

A Change of Fortune

When Danny was nine years old, he threw a grapefruit at Max that ended up hurtling out the living room window into the street below, landing with a thud a few feet from an old lady who was out walking her dog. When the apartment doorbell rang a few minutes later, Harold Gurkin found himself face to face with a yapping Chihuahua covered in grapefruit pulp and a fist-waving grandmother promising to call the police.

Danny was grounded for a week.

At ten, Danny lost television privileges for a month for pretending to have a temperature by holding the thermometer up to a lightbulb by his bed when his mother wasn't looking. After a couple of days of school-less bliss, the plan came apart when he left the thermometer too long and it showed a fever of 107.

"You should be dead," Mrs. Gurkin had said, concern vanishing from her face. "And you will be when I tell your father what you've been up to!"

That wasn't pretty, and there had been other incidents as well. Who could forget the Flaming Macaroni Fiasco, the Antique Chair Leg Disaster, or the Missing Chocolate Cake Conspiracy? And those were just in the last three months.

But Danny had never seen his parents this angry. What would the punishment be this time? Locked in his room with no television for a year? Dishwashing duty until the end of time? Maybe Max's suggestion—hanging—wouldn't be so bad. At least it would be quick!

Danny lay on his bed with his feet crossed against the wall, next to a yellowing newspaper front page that read SLUGGERS CLIMB OUT OF LAST PLACE!

He was still wearing the grease-covered EL SID T-shirt from the long journey, and his legs and arms ached. His head was throbbing from the sun, and his mouth was as dry as sandpaper.

He had never had a day go so right and so wrong all at once. It was hard to believe it had all happened. The long road trip. The Boddlebrooks mansion with its fifty-two spectacular bedrooms. Seymour Sycamore and his creepy wandering eye. The amazing study and the hidden passageway. The baseball-bat tower and the secret gum!

Danny reached into his pocket and pulled out the three packets of gum, turning them over in his fingers like a jeweler examining a diamond.

It was amazing to think that something from the Boddlebrooks mansion could actually exist in his room. But the gum was real, and the words still leapt off the packets.

"Longest-Lasting Kosmic Kranberry—Manchester E. Boddlebrooks's 53rd Exciting Flavor."

In the rush to leave the mansion, Danny hadn't had time to tell Molly or Lucas what he had found. He could have said something to them during the trip home—and he almost did several times—but he kept quiet instead.

Maybe it was selfish, but Danny liked the idea of having a secret that only he and Manchester Boddlebrooks shared.

Danny ran his finger along the edge of one of the packets. He was dying to open the gum, but he kept telling himself he should resist. The antique packets were souvenirs of the greatest adventure he'd ever had. They were a part of Sluggers history. They were a bridge across time to Manchester Boddlebrooks himself!

"I will treasure them forever! I will never open them!" Danny said to himself, placing the gum on the bed beside him and nodding in admiration at his own restraint.

Danny hit the button on the clock radio by his bed, and the sounds of WBUB, the Sluggers station, filled the room. He always kept his radio tuned to WBUB. It was 7:35 and the game was just half an hour old, but the team was already down 2–0 to the Charleston Bruisers.

"That's what happens when you miss the first pitch," Danny thought.

He grabbed the cordless phone by the side of the bed and punched in the first six digits of Molly's number, then hung up. He began dialing Lucas's number but chickened out again.

What if Molly and Lucas already knew that he had broken under interrogation? What would they think of him? What would they *do* to him?

Come to think of it, Danny dreaded the prospect of ever seeing his friends again. Of course, it probably wouldn't be an issue since they were all going to be grounded for the next twenty-five to thirty years.

"We move to the bottom of the fifth inning, and as

usual, these Sluggers just can't catch a break. They're down three—nothing with just two hits between them. Another miserable performance," said the Sluggers' radio announcer Marv Maxwell.

Danny picked up the gum again, his eyes focusing on the intricate bubble-gum-tycoon constellation.

"Oh, I'll just open one pack," Danny decided. He could save the other two for posterity.

He tore back the end of one of the packets and found eight sticks of gum inside, each covered in thin white paper. He pulled out a stick and unwrapped it slowly, the tangy smell of concentrated cranberries filling his nose.

Danny had been so excited about finding the secret gum that he had completely forgotten one important fact.

He hated cranberries!

He hated them more than liver. He hated them more than Brussels sprouts. He hated them more than anchovies. Come to think of it, he hated them more than Max, though that was a close call.

When Danny was in the third grade, he'd had to write a school paper about his least favorite food, and he'd picked the cranberry.

He'd learned, among other things, that the first cranberries had sprung up about ten thousand years before and only grew in the smelliest marshlands of prehistoric North America. The marshes were so damp and putrid that they sent the dinosaurs running for cover, which was saying something because the dinosaurs probably didn't smell like roses themselves.

Over thousands of years, all sorts of tiny insects and bugs and other disgusting creatures got trapped and died in the marshlands, and through some awful miracle, the first cranberry vines popped up out of all that mess.

Never had a food that had taken so much effort to create tasted so awful, Danny thought.

That the cranberry became part of Thanksgiving dinner, to be consumed every year by countless families until the end of time, was clearly a sick joke played on the Pilgrims by the Native Americans. At least, that was what Danny had written in his paper. He'd gotten a C.

"Well, Marv, we have mercifully reached the bottom of the ninth inning, and with the Sluggers down four–nothing, there's little doubt about the outcome," said the team's other radio announcer, Chad Carson. *"I know I've said this many times before, but I think this just might be a new low for the Sluggers. They look like they've all been run through a car wash or something. There's no energy there!"*

First up for the Sluggers was a rookie named Sam Slasky, who had struck out seventeen times in a row, just two shy of the big-league record.

"Oooh . . . high and outside," Marv Maxwell said. *"Hey, but did you see that? Slasky didn't swing at it. That's a rare moment."*

"Rare is right," Danny thought. Slasky was by far the Sluggers' dumbest hitter. He would swing at anything, and opposing pitchers knew it, so they never threw him any good pitches to hit. Once he'd even struck out between innings! Danny couldn't remember the last time Slasky had drawn a walk.

"Ball four!" Carson said with surprise. *"Slasky is walking to first base!"*

Danny fiddled with the bright red stick of gum in his hand. He couldn't *not* see what it tasted like, but the thought of eating century-old cranberries filled him with dread.

"Oh, what have I got to lose," Danny thought. "Anything made by Manchester Boddlebrooks can't be that bad!"

He held his nose, opened his mouth, and started chewing. It was a mistake! The gum was so tart it forced him to suck in his cheeks. Worse, it had a strange fizz to it, bursting in little pops of cranberry revulsion on the tip of his tongue.

"And Chuck Sidewinder lines a sharp single to center!" Marv Maxwell yelled. *"Sakes alive, Chad! Slasky is rounding second and going all the way to third base! Ladies and gentlemen, I kid you not. The Sluggers have*

men on first and third with nobody out. How about that?"

"Yes!" Danny shouted, punching his fist in the air. This was getting good. He heard his father and Max pounding against the sofa in the next room.

Danny was tempted to run out and join the others, but he stopped himself. He wouldn't give them the satisfaction! Anyway, whatever he was doing in his bedroom prison cell was working, so maybe it was better this way.

He leaned forward and turned up the volume.

The next batter was Boom-Boom Bigersley, a former monk who started playing first base for the Sluggers after he was kicked out of a monastery for making too much noise. He was convinced he'd been cursed because of his failure, and had resolved ever since then to let his bat speak for him whenever possible.

"And that's a long fly ball by Boom-Boom. It's going way, way, way back . . . ," Carson screamed. *"It's off the top of the center field wall. Did you see that? Of course you didn't, this is radio, but take my word for it! Call your aunt Edna in Florida! Bigersley has a triple and the Sluggers have just scored two runs. It's four to two, folks. Why, that's the first time Boom-Boom has hit a ball out of the infield since July twenty-second!"*

"Wooohoooo!" Danny shrieked. He was standing on the bed now, bouncing up and down. The Sluggers were back in the game!

Sluggers shortstop P. J. Planter was next, and Danny plopped back down on the bed and went into his lucky yoga position. He blew a cranberry bubble.

Planter walked on four pitches in the dirt from the rattled Bruisers pitcher, Tug Johnson.

"Bruisers manager Sebastian St. Croix is out at the mound to calm down Johnson," Marv Maxwell said, his tinny voice hard to hear over the buzz of the crowd. *"Johnson looks like a man who's just been told his house is on fire. He looks livid. This could get interesting."*

"Tug Johnson must have been expecting a cakewalk against the Sluggers," Danny thought. Now he was on the ropes. Men on first and third base, still nobody out!

The crowd moaned as second baseman Spanky Mazoo walked to the plate. Mazoo was one of those players everybody loved to hate. He never talked to reporters, refused to stay at the same hotel as the rest of the team, and had a contract that allowed him to take his personal trainer, massage therapist, and accountant with him wherever he went. He was supposed to be the Sluggers' best player, but he never seemed to try very hard.

Danny stuck the gum between his front teeth as Johnson delivered the first pitch to Mazoo.

Clunk!

"Would you look at that?" Carson marveled. *"Mazoo has been hit by the pitch. That's going to load the*

bases with Sluggers. I can't remember the last time I said that."

"That had to hurt," Maxwell added. "You know, that's the first time I've seen Mazoo use his head all year. He took one for the team there. His accountant has got to be nervous."

The bases loaded! The Sluggers down just 4–2! Nobody out in the bottom of the ninth inning!

Danny decided to hold his breath until the next batter batted or until he passed out. Whichever came first! He took the gum out of his mouth and held it in his hand, then breathed in sharply and closed his eyes. What a relief it was to be free of the taste of cranberries, Danny thought. He could see why Manchester had never released his fifty-third flavor. It never would have sold.

"Ooh, that's strike one on the inside corner . . . ," Maxwell said.

"Strike two, right down the pike . . .

"Swing and a miss! Swing and a miss!" Maxwell said. "Tito Calagara goes down swinging, and that's one out."

"No!" Danny moaned. "Say it ain't so, Tito!"

Danny put a pencil under his nose for good luck as Sluggers left fielder Bruce Minsky stepped to the plate. He took in another sharp breath.

"Johnson has the sign from his catcher and he's ready

to deliver the pitch. Boy, he looks mean. He's screaming something at Minsky, but I'm not sure what he said, Marv," Carson said. "Probably better if we don't repeat it anyway."

Danny scrunched his nose down on the pencil as hard as he could.

"Here's the windup and the pitch . . . ," Maxwell said. "Oh no! Minsky pops out. That was not a good time to have a bad at bat. That's two away."

"The bases are still loaded, but the team is down to its final out. It looks like the Sluggers are about to waste one of their best chances of the season," Carson moaned.

Danny slammed his fist down on the bed. He had been squeezing the Kosmic Kranberry gum in his palm, and now it was stuck to his fingers like a web.

He bit the gum off his fingers with his teeth and gobbled it into his mouth. The taste made him shudder.

The Sluggers' last hope was Thelonius Star, the team's tiny right fielder. Star was so small locker-room attendants would sometimes mistake him for the ball boy, but now he held the game in his hands.

"The crowd is on its feet—men, women, and children cheering like mad," Maxwell said. "You know, Chad, I've been in this business for thirty-four years, but it still hurts to see them get so excited when you know the Sluggers are just going to let them down. It's depressing."

"I know what you mean, Marv, but you never know,"

said Carson. *"The Sluggers might just win a game one of these days."*

Both men laughed.

Danny didn't think it was funny.

As the Bruisers' pitcher got ready to deliver, the crowd screamed and stomped on their chairs. Danny held his hands together, his fingers locked in prayer.

"Here's the pitch from Johnson . . . ," Maxwell said in a whisper.

Crack!

Even over the radio, even with the crowd on its feet, Danny needed no announcer to tell him what that sound meant. It was the sweetest sound in the world. The sound of leather hitting the purest part of the bat.

"Star's hit the ball. He's crushed it into the night sky!" Marv Maxwell screamed, his voice cracking. *"That ball ain't coming back! Home run! Home run! Thelonius Star has hit a grand-slam home run! Six to four! Six to four! The Sluggers have won the ball game! The Sluggers have won! They've won!"*

Who Won It for the Sluggers?

Danny pulled open his bedroom door the next morning and crept out to the kitchen. It didn't matter that he would soon find out what punishment his parents had in store for him. It didn't matter that he had tossed and turned all night, unable to shake off a dream in which he was imprisoned in a dungeon by the evil Captain Cranberry, overlord of the planet Tart.

The Sluggers were on a one-game winning streak, and that meant that the world was a wonderful place.

Still, he approached the kitchen slowly. His mother was sitting at the table with her back to the door, reading the newspaper and nibbling on an English muffin. Danny stopped at the doorway and peered in at her.

Any kid facing the Grand Canyon of punishments will tell you that you should never sneak up on a potentially dangerous parent without first getting a good read on his or her mood. Parents can be unpredictable, and caution is key. But from his position in the doorway, it was hard — even for an experienced parent observer like Danny — to tell whether his mother was still angry.

He sidled over to the fridge and reached inside for a carton of orange juice, trying to make himself as small as possible.

"What a game, huh!" Danny's mother exclaimed.

In the Gurkin family, some things were more important than handing out punishments, even extra-large, bubble-gum-tycoon-sized punishments like the one Danny expected.

A dramatic come-from-behind victory by the

Sluggers in the bottom of the ninth inning on a grand slam by the smallest player on the team pretty much overrode anything else that might have happened in the preceding twenty-four hours.

Danny closed the refrigerator and turned around. His mother held up the newspaper so Danny could see the headline on the back page.

STAR-STRUCK! it read, above a full-page photo of Thelonius Star swinging with all his might. If you looked closely at the photograph, you could see that his eyes were closed. The newspaper also noted that the Sluggers were still sixteen games out of first place.

"I'll tell you a secret," Lydia Gurkin said. "I won the game for the Sluggers!"

"What's that, Mom?" Danny asked, taking a seat at the table across from her.

"It was me. In the bottom of the ninth inning, I figured they needed a little extra help, so I got up and started washing the dishes. They weren't even dirty. I just rewashed clean ones. That always seems to help," his mother said. "The second I started washing, they started their rally!"

Danny was taken aback. Sure, he was aware of the extraordinary things that could happen when his mother stopped watching a game and left the room. It always helped the team. Everyone in the family agreed on that.

But Danny was fairly certain that *he* had won the game for the Sluggers.

It was he who had held his breath, scrunched his nose against a pencil, become a baseball yoga master, and popped a wad of century-old gum into his mouth. Surely he had done more than anyone to take the Sluggers to victory.

But Danny didn't want to be rude, so he didn't say anything.

"I have to admit, it wasn't the same watching the game without the Sluggers' biggest fan," Mrs. Gurkin said, reaching over and ruffling Danny's hair. "But what you and your friends did yesterday was very dangerous and very stupid."

"Yeah, I guess," Danny said.

"We'd be bad parents if we didn't punish you for it," his mother continued.

"I wouldn't be so hard on yourselves," Danny offered.

Danny's mother put the newspaper down on the table and looked at him.

"You know, last night your father and I agreed on a punishment for you," she said. "Grounded and no television until school starts."

"Grounded *and* no television!" Danny exclaimed. It was unnatural.

"But . . . ," she continued, "after the game we had a

long talk. You wouldn't believe some of the crazy things your father did for that team when he was younger. Why, there was the time he ran away from home to try to win a job as the Sluggers' ball boy, the time he sold your grandfather's car in exchange for season tickets, and the time he parachuted onto the field during the national anthem."

Parachuted onto the field! Danny hadn't heard that one.

"In any case, we're upset that you lied to us, and we're upset you would do something as dumb as what you did," Danny's mother said. "But Gurkins have always done stupid things for the Sluggers. It's a family tradition."

This was much better than Danny could have hoped for. It was amazing how a simple win by the Sluggers could make everything brighter. Imagine what a championship would do!

"So does that mean I'm not punished?" Danny asked.

"Oh, we still have a punishment for you, I'm afraid," Mrs. Gurkin said. "Well, more of a favor than a punishment. Actually, more of an order than a favor. It involves your aunt Betty."

"Oh no!"

"Yes, I'm afraid it does," his mother went on. "You see, your father has promised to help her move next weekend, but he really can't with the campaign in full swing. He thought you might want to do it for him, as a way of making it up to us."

"What about Max? Is he coming?" Danny asked. Danny's aunt Betty was all right, but her two kids, Gertrude and Philip, were awful, and Danny couldn't stomach seeing them alone.

"Not exactly," his mother said.

"Why not?" Danny asked. "Why does he get out of it?"

"Well, mostly because Max didn't almost get himself and his friends killed yesterday by taking a bike ride on the Harry Tinkleford Highway," his mother said.

"This is so unfair!" Danny protested, but he knew he was in no position to push it.

"Danny, who ever told you that life was fair?" his mother replied with a smile. "No Sluggers fan I know would say a thing like that."

A Knock at the Door

On a moonlit night in 1934, Skidmore Boddlebrooks opened the heavy front door to his bayside mansion in East Bubble to find himself staring into the eyes of a stooped old man. The man was clutching a small suitcase in one hand and a flimsy cardboard box in the other, and he seemed to have come out of nowhere.

"Can I help you?" said Skidmore, leaning against the doorframe with a cigar in his mouth and a crystal glass filled with bourbon in his right hand. His hair had grayed in the decades since the pretzel tragedy, and his face was creased by thin wrinkles.

Inside, Skidmore's party was going strong. Jazz music from a quartet Skidmore had hired wafted out the door and into the night. Skidmore had been in the middle of telling a joke to the governor when he'd heard the doorbell ring.

"Are you all right, sir?" Skidmore asked brusquely. "Are you in some sort of trouble?"

Skidmore did not like being taken away from his party, and he especially didn't like being interrupted in the middle of telling a joke to the governor. He considered himself a man of respect and breeding, and he was one of the wealthiest people in the country. Sure, he still owned a terrible baseball team that he'd inherited from his dead brother, but he had many other businesses as well.

Good businesses, like the Twisty-Doughy Pretzel Co., Inc., which boasted five thousand warehouses around the country, each filled to the rooftop with piles of pretzels.

Successful businesses like the Ball-Park Mustard Goo Conglomerate, which produced enough extra-spicy mustard each year to flood the Mississippi, the Amazon, and the Yangtze, or so Skidmore had been told by his managers. Certainly that was a lot of mustard, and anyone who could produce it was not someone to be trifled with.

Who was this little man at the door, and what was he doing intruding on his night? Skidmore thought.

"I came about the ad," the man said. His voice was thin, but it held a listener's attention, even a listener as important as Skidmore Boddlebrooks. "About the caretaker you're looking for for your brother's mansion."

"Well, that's lovely, sir, but it's after midnight right now. Why don't you come around to my office in the morning and we can discuss it?" Skidmore said. He gave the man a hard look.

"I'll take the job," the old man said, meeting his stare. "I'm going to move in tonight."

Skidmore paused. He wasn't used to being talked to like this. He swirled the ice around in his drink and took a puff on his cigar. There was something familiar about the man, but Skidmore couldn't put his finger on it. He was sure that he had never seen him before in his life. He would have remembered someone like this.

"We can talk about it in the morning," Skidmore said nervously.

"We can talk about it at the house after I move in," the old man said matter-of-factly. "Why don't you come by one morning any time after ten o'clock."

And with that, the little man turned his back on Skidmore and shuffled quickly down the drive. Skidmore Boddlebrooks stood in the light of the doorway and stared after him, a thin trail of smoke rising from his cigar and the ice melting slowly in his drink.

The Reckoning

Danny shot out his front door and down the stairs, on his way to Quincy Park and what he figured was almost certain doom. He might have gotten off easy with his mother, but he certainly wasn't going to be so lucky with Molly and Lucas. After all, parents pretty much have to forgive you eventually since you all live together and you're related and everything. Friends have more options.

Of course, if Molly and Lucas were grounded, they might not be at the park. Danny could only hope.

Danny strode through the park gate with his heart in his throat. He looked around at the crowds of children.

There were a few girls from school hanging out on a bench, and some seventh graders shooting hoops at the farthest court.

The whole walk over from Chorloff Street, Danny had been rehearsing ways of apologizing, but none seemed adequate. He had dragged his two best friends on a grueling bike ride to West Bubble, insisted on making them late getting back by sneaking into Boddlebrooks's study, and then snitched about the whole thing.

He was pathetic! What could he say?

Danny spotted Lucas first, walking down a gravel path toward the basketball courts about twenty feet away. Lucas was coming straight at him. Then he saw Molly. She was approaching from the other direction, bouncing a basketball with the tips of her fingers, her Sluggers cap pulled low over her face.

Danny waved meekly at both of them, but neither

responded. Maybe they hadn't seen him. Both were looking down at the ground.

He considered making a run for it, then realized that would probably be the lamest thing anyone in the world had ever done.

"Hey, Lucas," Danny said, looking down at his shoes. "Hey, Mol."

"Hey," Lucas said sheepishly.

"Hey, Danny. Hey, Doughboy," Molly whispered.

There was dead silence.

Danny couldn't take it. They *hated* him. His stomach was churning.

"I'm so sorry!" Danny blurted, and was surprised to hear the exact same words come out of his two friends' mouths.

"You're sorry?" Danny said.

"But I . . . ," said Molly.

"Huh?" said Lucas.

Everyone laughed.

"I lasted five minutes before I crumbled," Molly said. "I just couldn't stop myself. I tried the cat-down-the-manhole story, but my mother saw right through me. She said if the next thing out of my mouth wasn't the truth, I'd be in three times as much trouble. I'm sorry. I blabbed."

Then it was Lucas's turn.

"I actually had my parents going there for a while

with the story about being hit on the head by a beam and losing my memory," he said. "But then they insisted on taking me to the hospital to see a brain specialist, so I just came out and told them the truth. I figured if someone could look into my brain, they'd probably be able to see what really happened anyway."

"Doughboy, you really are an idiot!" Molly said. "They can't see into your brain!"

Danny told his friends about his own performance. He was so relieved.

"So weren't either of you punished? I figured you'd be grounded forever, Lucas," Danny said.

"Oh, I was punished, and it was much worse than being grounded," Lucas said. "I have to wash my parents' ugly car once a week for six months, and . . . I have to take piano lessons!"

"What? That's the stupidest punishment I've ever heard," Danny said. "Why piano lessons?"

"My parents are very cruel people, Danny," Lucas said. "I think one time many years ago I said that the thing I would hate most in the world would be piano lessons. They must have written it down somewhere and just waited."

"What about you, Molly?" Danny asked.

"Actually, I'm not in trouble at all," she said. "But my mother said that I am supposed to tell you, 'You are a bad influence, Daniel Gurkin.'"

"I guess I am," Danny laughed.

They sat down on a park bench and discussed every pitch of the Sluggers game, especially the home run.

"What a shot!" Molly said. "And did you see that pitch to Mazoo? That thing hit him square in the head."

"You know," Lucas said, leaning over on the bench as if he had a secret to share and turning his head from Molly to Danny. "I won the game for them."

"Say that again?" Danny said.

"I won the game for the Sluggers," Lucas explained. "I watched the entire ninth inning with the volume turned down on the television, and it worked."

Danny couldn't believe his ears. Some people!

First his mother and now Lucas. Could there be any doubt who had *really* won the game for the Sluggers? But Danny kept quiet.

"And I dedicate my victory to my late bicycle," Lucas continued. "It perished for a noble cause." Molly and Danny took off their caps and put their hands over their hearts in mock respect.

Sizzling Sid Canova

Sid Canova was nervous. He paced around the back of the mound. He rubbed the ball in his hands. He took his cap off and talked to himself.

Finally, the young pitcher strode onto the mound, placed his right foot on the pitching rubber, and looked in toward the batter.

Straight into the television camera. Straight into Danny's living room.

Danny was lying on his back on the floor, directly in front of the television, his head resting on a pillow he'd grabbed from the couch. Lucas had draped himself over the easy chair Max usually went for, and Molly was sitting on the edge of the couch. Each had a half-eaten hot dog in one hand, the remains of a hasty order from Willie's cart.

Danny had insisted.

"I'm sorry to be bossy," he'd said on the walk over from Quincy Park. "But with Canova on the mound, we can't take any chances."

As Willie topped the hot dogs with onion goop, Danny, Molly, and Lucas told him about the trip to the Boddlebrooks mansion.

"You say there were doors shaped like hot dogs, a room covered in sauerkraut, and an old geezer with eyes that went off in different directions?" Willie asked after they had finished the story. "Now, that I've got to see."

"You should make up your apartment like that," Lucas said. "You know, with hot-dog doors and sauerkraut wallpaper."

"Oh, I don't know, Lucas," Willie said. "When I'm not selling hot dogs, I like to do other things. I don't think I'd want to take my work home with me."

"Yeah, I can see that," Lucas replied, stuffing the corner of the first hot dog into his mouth. He gobbled up a strand of sauerkraut that was left dangling from his lip.

Danny had called his mother from a pay phone and was surprised when she'd suggested he bring his friends over for the game. He wasn't sure if it was a peace offering or an attempt to get the three accomplices together in one room.

Canova shook off the first three signs from the Sluggers' catcher, Chico Medley. He was already perspiring, and the game hadn't even started.

"Come on, Sid!" Lucas yelled from the easy chair. "Let's go! Two in a row!"

Finally, Canova delivered the first pitch, serving up a fat fastball right down the middle of the plate. He might as well have walked it over on a platter with some eggs and bacon for Bruisers batter Finnigan Clark, who crushed the ball right back toward the mound.

"Look out, Mary! Base hit up the middle," said Bullet Santana, the Sluggers' television announcer. Canova was no longer staring in at the camera. He was sprawled on the mound with his feet up in the air and a look of terror in his eyes.

"That ball almost took his head off," said Santana's partner, Wally Mandelberg. *"Folks, if Canova seems distracted, it's because he just saw his young life flash before his eyes. Give him some space."*

"Whoa! That was a close one," Molly said.

"Not a good start," Danny admitted.

"Ugly," said Lucas.

Canova gave up another hit, and then another and another. Nothing he threw seemed to be fooling anybody. The Bruisers batters sprayed the ball all over the field as if they were playing tennis.

"How do you like that, folks? The Sluggers are already down two to nothing and my seat isn't even warm yet," Santana said. *"Canova looks rattled out there."*

The young pitcher slammed his mitt into his thigh and stared up at the sky. He held the baseball up to his face and started shouting at it as manager Finchley Biggins and the Sluggers infielders huddled around him for a meeting.

"What do you think they're saying to him, Bullet?" Mandelberg asked.

"Well, I don't think they're making dinner plans!" Santana quipped. *"Somebody ought to hold up a couple of fingers and make sure that kid can still see straight."*

"You guys, put your baseball caps on backward," Danny instructed Molly and Lucas. "Sid needs some help."

Danny got up and went into each room in the apartment, pushing down on the windows to make sure they were all closed firmly. He didn't want anything to jinx Canova.

His mother was in the kitchen drying her hands.

"I'm just coming in to watch," she said, before noticing the look on Danny's face. "Or do you think I should do some dishes first instead?"

"I think dishes," Danny said. "Lots of dishes."

Danny had one more window to check. He pressed open the door to his room and stepped inside. The window was indeed open, and Danny pushed down on the sash until it was closed tightly.

"That ought to do it," he thought, and turned to go back to the others.

Danny was about to close the bedroom door behind him when he stopped in his tracks. He slipped back into the room, reached under his mattress, and pulled out the Kosmic Kranberry.

It had only been twenty-four hours since the amazing trip to Boddlebrooks's mansion, but it already seemed like a dream. He just wanted to take a quick peek at the star-spattered packet to make sure it was really there.

Before he knew it, Danny had unpeeled another stick of gum and slipped it in his mouth. He puckered his lips as the awful taste oozed over his tongue. Then he got up and scurried back into the living room.

"What's that smell, dude?" Lucas asked almost immediately. "It smells like Thanksgiving dinner or something."

"Oh, just some gum," Danny said, trying to sound as casual as possible. "Sorry, I only have one piece."

Canova had somehow managed to get out of the inning while Danny was away, but the Sluggers were down 3–0. Lydia Gurkin had washed all the dishes twice and came in to watch, sitting down next to Molly on the sofa.

Sam Slasky led off the bottom of the first inning for the Sluggers, and the television flashed his statistics — a .237 batting average with just two home runs and fourteen runs batted in. Not exactly the kind of numbers that will get you into the Hall of Fame. But Slasky had stopped his run of strikeouts at seventeen the night before, so things were looking up.

The Bruisers pitcher was a hard-throwing kid from Wyoming named Brockton Kern. He was blond and beefy, like a lifeguard, and he threw the ball just one way.

Fast.

In the off-season, Kern had been on a safari in Kenya when a 280-pound lion charged out of the bushes straight at him. Kern was unarmed except for a baseball he always kept in his jacket pocket. Suffice it to say, the lion was now a rug at Brockton Kern's summer house.

And Slasky was no lion.

Bang!

"Did you see that?" shouted Mandelberg. *"He hit it! And not only that, he crushed it!"*

The ball shot off Slasky's bat like a rocket and out toward the center field wall. The Bruisers center fielder ran toward the wall and leapt in the air, but he had no chance. The ball settled into the stands, ten rows back.

"Home run!" Danny cheered.

"Yahooooooooo!" screamed Molly, Lucas, and Mrs. Gurkin.

Kern looked stunned. No 152-pound weakling like Slasky had ever touched him for a home run, certainly none that played for the Sluggers, the worst team in baseball.

It was inconceivable.

It was 3–1.

But Slasky's home run was only the beginning. Chuck Sidewinder doubled. Boom-Boom Bigersley singled him home. P. J. Planter laid down a surprise bunt base hit, and Spanky Mazoo smashed another home run to make it 5–3 Sluggers.

Brockton Kern suddenly seemed two feet shorter. His massive chest had deflated, and his eyes held a look of utter confusion.

"That lion must have been a pussycat," Danny thought with delight as he, Molly, and Lucas waggled their arms in front of their chests like zombies.

In the second inning, Canova mowed down the Bruisers one-two-three, and after that the Sluggers went back on the attack, knocking Kern around like a piñata.

By the sixth inning it was 14–3, and every Sluggers player had at least two hits. Kern was long gone by then, having showered and left the stadium for an emergency phone session with his psychologist.

Canova, on the other hand, seemed to be getting stronger with every batter. When he came out for the ninth inning with the Sluggers up 19–3, the crowd gave him a huge ovation. Danny, Molly, Lucas, and Mrs. Gurkin were standing too, their voices hoarse from all the cheering they'd been doing.

"Mow 'em down, Sid!" Lucas screamed after the first batter struck out.

"Take us home!" Molly yelled as the second batter fanned too.

"One more to go!" Lydia Gurkin shouted as the last Bruisers batter, Bill Bagwell, stepped to the plate.

"Folks, we are on the verge of history here," Santana gushed. *"The Sluggers haven't scored nineteen runs in a game since 1957, and they lost that game twenty-three to nineteen! Heck, they go months sometimes without scoring nineteen runs combined."*

"You know, Bullet, I've been pinching myself all night," Mandelberg said. *"I keep thinking the alarm clock is going to go off and I'll wake up and be an announcer for the worst team in baseball again instead of for a team that's about to win two in a row. This is uncharted territory!"*

The two announcers ran through the big-league scoreboard. The Tornadoes had lost, so the Sluggers were on the verge of picking up another game. They would still be fifteen games out of first place, but at least they were heading in the right direction.

The stadium crowd was on its feet as Canova turned his attention to Bagwell and delivered.

"Strike one!" screamed the umpire.

Bagwell stepped out of the batter's box and rubbed his eyes. How could Canova still be throwing this hard after nine innings?

"Strike two!"

Even Canova looked a little surprised at how much velocity he'd gotten on the ball. One strike to go.

This time Canova threw a curveball. Not just any curveball, however. This was a thing of beauty, starting in at Bagwell's head and then biting sharply toward the plate as if it were on a string. It hit Chico Medley's mitt with a thump. Bagwell didn't even wait for the umpire's call before he started walking back to the dugout.

"STRIKE THREE!" the umpire screamed, jabbing

his right hand in the air like an exclamation point.

"The Sluggers have done it again! That's two in a row," Santana shouted. *"My friends, get out your dictionaries and turn to the back. I think that's where you'll find the definition of a winning streak!"*

The New Caretaker

It took several weeks for Skidmore Boddlebrooks to get the courage up to visit his dead brother's mansion, though he had heard reports that the old man who had interrupted his party had already made himself at home, cleaning and dusting every room of the massive house.

Strangely, the Sluggers had been playing well ever since the man had moved in. The team was in first place for the first time in nearly thirty years, and they looked to be heading for a pennant. That summer, the summer of 1934, was shaping up to be perhaps the most glorious in memory. The sun shone nearly every day, the sky was a deep and satisfying blue, and Winning Streak Stadium was packed to the last seat.

It was a time of great optimism, and great profits.

Skidmore's driver held open the door of the mustard yellow Rolls-Royce and stood at attention as his boss got out of the car. Skidmore scowled as he glanced up at the enormous double hot-dog doors, the round windows, and the baseball-bat towers of the impossibly red building in front of him.

"What a monstrosity," he mumbled to himself as he made his way to the door. "I should have torn this place down long ago."

Skidmore grabbed hold of one of the enormous S-shaped knockers and banged impatiently. He wanted to get this over with.

He stood and waited.

He looked at his watch.

"Who is it?" said a voice from an upstairs window. "Do you have an appointment?"

"I say! This is Skidmore Boddlebrooks. Open this door at once," Skidmore huffed, leaning an arm on the wood frame and rapping his walking stick against the ground.

When the door didn't open immediately, Skidmore knocked again.

"Yes, yes. Hold your horses," said the voice, but it was several minutes before the door creaked open, and Skidmore found himself standing once again face to face with the stooped old gentleman. He looked the same, except this time he was chewing a stick of extremely smelly gum.

Skidmore scrunched up his nose in disgust. He couldn't help noting that their roles had reversed, with the old man standing inside the doorway of the great house looking out at him. It was not a feeling Skidmore appreciated, especially since he'd never actually given the man the job of caretaker. How had this happened? Skidmore thought.

"I've been expecting you," said the old man, looking his visitor up and down disapprovingly. "What took you so long?"

Skidmore almost fell backward. He had promised himself that he would not allow this strange little man to get the better of him.

"You are a mustard millionaire. You are a man of consequence. What are you afraid of?" Skidmore had asked himself in the mirror that very morning as a servant buffed and polished his mustard yellow shoes.

But standing eyeball to eyeball with the man, Skidmore again found it hard to stand firm.

"Sir, this is my mansion, after all," Skidmore said. "I can come and go as I please, don't you think?"

"It's Manchester Boddlebrooks's mansion," said the old man flatly.

The impertinence! Skidmore was of half a mind to chuck the old man out, but he couldn't get the words out of his mouth. They stuck in his throat in a way that was most unbecoming of a man of such vast wealth.

"Well, Mr. . . . What did you say your name was?" Skidmore asked. It was all he could manage.

"I didn't," said the man.

"Well, what is your name?" Skidmore said impatiently.

The man lifted his head as high as he could, so that for the first time he was staring directly into Skidmore's eyes. He was actually quite tall when he uncoiled his body, and not nearly as old as he appeared when bent over. He might even have been younger than Skidmore himself, but there was a long history written in the lines of the man's forehead, and some unknowable story in the glint of his one good eye.

"My name? Errrr . . . well, that would be, ah . . . um," said the man, his wandering eye scanning the line of trees on the edge of the driveway behind Skidmore, who was so mesmerized by the man's face that he was barely listening.

"The name's Sycamore," the caretaker said finally. "Seymour Sycamore."

On a Roll

After the game against the Bruisers, the Sluggers went on a roll the likes of which had not been seen in seventy-two years. They flew out west and swept the Oakland Ogres 11–2, 15–3, and 8–0, then destroyed the Minnesota Muckrakers 12–4, 8–1, and 17–0.

Danny had been a superstitious fan long enough to know that you don't mess with success. Something he was doing was working, and Danny made sure he stuck with it. He wore his grimy EL SID shirt, avoided stepping on a single crack in the sidewalk, kept up his regimen of two hot dogs with everything, and started chewing the Kosmic Kranberry for every pitch.

The Sluggers climbed out of last place that Saturday evening, or as it was better known in the Gurkin household, the Night Before the Day Before School Starts.

The next day was promptly declared a Day of Sluggabration by Mayor Fred Frompovich. The mayor ordered all police, bus drivers, and firemen to wear Sluggers caps instead of their normal headgear, and reserved the highest flagpole at City Hall for a thirty-foot-high replica of the Sluggers' only World Series banner. That last bit had been Danny's idea, and he was thrilled when his father suggested it to the mayor.

"In this city, Danny, a politician can never be too big a Sluggers fan," Harold Gurkin said with a sly smile.

Frompovich's opponent tried to get in on the act, swearing that as mayor he would build a new stadium and attend every game in it, but he couldn't match the mayor's enthusiasm. With less than two months to go until election day, Frompovich was now slightly ahead in the polls, and most of his advisers said it was due entirely to the Sluggers.

Danny wasn't alone in thinking his superstitions were behind the Sluggers' success. As the team won, people all over town started to come forward to claim that they had something to do with it.

A grandmother on Drew Street said she had started knitting a scarf on the day the winning streak started and wouldn't stop until the Sluggers won the World Series. A dentist on Park Way claimed the team had only begun playing well after he decided to fill cavities on the left sides of people's mouths on game days and make those with right-sided cavities wait until off days. A university professor swore the secret was his simultaneous translation of all Sluggers broadcasts into a little-known dialect of Cantonese.

Simply put, the city had caught Sluggers fever.

College students vowed not to bathe until the team was in first place. Construction workers got watermelon red Sluggers tattoos etched into their arms. Restaurants concocted dishes they promised would bring good luck: chicken Thelonius, mashed potato Mazoo, and spaghetti à la Sid Canova, among others.

All over the city, people held their heads higher. Their eyes were a little brighter, and their chests a bit fuller with pride. If losing was a disease, than the long-suffering Sluggers faithful had finally found the cure.

Still, catching the Texas Tornadoes would take a miracle. The Sluggers were eleven games out of first place with only nineteen games left in the season. Even making the play-offs as a wild-card team would be next to impossible, with most of the league still ahead of them.

Danny was sitting at the kitchen table reading the sports page and slurping down a bowl of cereal when the phone rang.

It may have been a Day of Sluggabration, but it was also the last morning before the doors at John J. Barnibus would swing open on a new school year and slam shut on a summer of freedom. It was the last day before Danny, Molly, and Lucas would be tossed under the treads of the Sherman Tank.

"What would you say if I told you I had tickets for the game against the Tornadoes tonight?" said the breathless voice on the other end of the phone.

It was Molly.

"I'd say, 'I'll kiss Mrs. Sherman on the lips and do your history homework for a year if you take me with you,'" Danny replied.

"That would be amusing but unnecessary," said Molly. "And I'm better than you at history anyway."

"This is true," Danny admitted. "Okay, you name it, I'll do it."

"Actually, you don't have to do anything. Just help my father with an article he's writing," Molly said. "He asked me who my most superstitious friend was, and of course I said you. He wants to interview you about the things you do to help the team, and he wants to do it from the press box. There's a pass for Lucas too."

"The press box!" Danny shouted. "That's the coolest thing ever."

"I told him about the hot dogs and the way you don't step on cracks in the sidewalk and all that stuff, and he's convinced you're even crazier than all the other people," Molly said. "He just kept saying, 'Perfect, perfect, perfect!'"

"Really? He said that?" Danny asked. "Do you think he meant perfect good or perfect bad?"

"I dunno," Molly said. "He just said 'perfect.'"

"Hmmm," Danny said. He wasn't sure whether to be flattered or insulted.

"Hey, Mol, who's pitching for the Tornadoes?" Danny asked.

"It's Ruffian," Molly replied. "And he's promised he's going to crush the Sluggers tonight. Actually, he said it with a Swedish accent, so it didn't sound that menacing, but he seemed to really mean it."

Winning Streak Stadium

There is something unspeakably beautiful about a big-league ball field, and the first glimpse is always the best. From the press box, Winning Streak Stadium stretched out before Danny like a painting, with its lush green grass, its rich brown base paths, and its vivid white foul lines. Danny was so close to the field that he could see the smile on Boom-Boom Bigersley's face as he joked with Sid Canova near the third baseline and hear Spanky Mazoo clear his throat before launching a giant wad of spit into short center field, as if fifty-five thousand people weren't piling into the stands to watch him.

It was perfect.

Ebenezer Gurkin, Danny's grandfather, had put it best when he took Danny to his first-ever Sluggers game at the age of three and a half.

"A baseball stadium isn't real life," Ebenezer had told Danny. "It's what real life should be."

Danny hadn't really understood what he meant at the time, partially because Grandpa Ebenezer's false teeth had fallen out in the middle of the sentence, and partially because Danny was so young. But he understood now.

The press box was a wide gallery with three long rows of desks, each raised slightly higher than the one in front. At each desk, dozens of reporters sat talking into cell phones and tapping away at laptop computers.

At the far end of the room was a table with five different types of soda, Gatorade, mineral water, piles of thick salami and tuna fish sandwiches, and bowls filled with enough peanuts, popcorn, and potato chips to feed an army.

"Wow!" Lucas had said when they entered, making his way immediately for the food.

The evening had begun an hour earlier with a pregame pilgrimage to Willie's cart, where Jim Fitch, Molly's father, did his best to get his head around the ins and outs of Danny's hot-dog rule book.

"Does it matter if any of the sauerkraut or the onion goop falls on the ground?" Mr. Fitch asked.

"Well, clearly, that wouldn't be good," Danny answered between bites.

"I see," said Mr. Fitch, scratching in his notebook. He was a bear of a man, well over six feet tall, with an athlete's build but an accountant's sense of precision, and he stared intently at Danny as he belted out his questions.

"What if you came here one day and, say, Willie wasn't around. Would you just go somewhere else for your hot dogs?" said Mr. Fitch, waving his pen in the air.

Danny thought for a minute.

"Willie's always here," he replied.

"I *am* always here," Willie concurred.

"Uh-huh," Mr. Fitch said. "Okay, last question. What kind of dogs are we talking about here? All-beef? Have you ever tried a blood sausage or a bratwurst? How about veggie franks?"

"I never thought about any of that, to be honest," Danny said. "But I'd guess anything in the hot-dog family would help the team, as long as Willie was the one serving it."

"Great," Mr. Fitch said, sticking the notebook in his back pocket. "We're done here."

Now that they were at the stadium, Mr. Fitch had a million more things he wanted to get cleared up. He watched Danny intently as Sluggers left-hander Vince Spagu took the mound and delivered the first pitch. Danny had never been asked so many questions in his life.

"Do you cross your feet right over left or left over right? Is there any remedy if you do step on a crack in the sidewalk by mistake? Have you ever passed out from holding your breath too long?"

It was relentless, and it made it impossible for Danny to sneak the piece of Kosmic Kranberry he had brought into his mouth. Danny still hadn't told anybody about what he'd found in the secret room, and he certainly wasn't going to start with a newspaperman like Mr. Fitch.

While Danny answered Mr. Fitch's questions, Molly and Lucas leaned out over the waist-high railing that overlooked the field, cheering for the Sluggers and screaming abuse at the Tornadoes.

"Hey, Magnus!" Lucas yelled down when Ruffian

came out in the bottom of the first inning. *"Du stinka!"*

"That's Swedish for 'You stink!'" he explained to Molly when she gave him a quizzical look. "I learned it on the Internet."

Spagu mowed down the Tornadoes in the first three innings without giving up a run. Unfortunately, Ruffian was doing the same thing to the Sluggers.

Danny showed Mr. Fitch each of his superstitions, sucking in his stomach to get the Sluggers out of a bases-loaded jam in the fourth inning, crossing his toes when Boom-Boom Bigersley tried to bunt for a base hit in the sixth, holding his breath to help Spanky Mazoo stay alive with two strikes on him in the seventh.

As he went through his repertoire, a small crowd of journalists gathered around him.

"You do all that *every* game?" one of the writers asked.

"Well, yeah, and then there are some things I can only do at home," Danny explained, describing how he sat upside down on the couch, closed the windows tight when Sid Canova pitched, fought with his brother, and helped his mother wash dishes in the kitchen.

By the bottom of the eighth there was still no score, and the crowd was growing restless.

No matter what Danny did—standing on one foot, holding his breath, crossing his fingers—the Sluggers couldn't get a rally going.

The only reason they were in the game at all was Spagu, a forty-one-year-old former supermarket clerk who had discovered a mean knuckleball while throwing produce around with some coworkers. Nobody had ever seen a guava bob and weave the way it did when it left Spagu's hand, and the desperate Sluggers had signed him up.

It wasn't until Mr. Fitch got up to take a call from his editors in the top of the ninth inning that Danny had a chance to stick the Kosmic Kranberry into his mouth.

A moment later, Spagu sent the last Tornado batter, Mungo McBust, down on strikes. The Sluggers had one more chance to win the game before it went into extra innings.

All around Danny, sportswriters were typing furiously, trying to figure out how to write their stories and calling their editors to tell them they might have to hold the newspapers because the night could go long. Nobody seemed to have time to actually watch the game.

"Danny, I notice you've started chewing that bubble gum pretty hard," Mr. Fitch said, sliding his cell phone into his jacket pocket. "Sure smells strange, that gum. Is that another one of your superstitions?"

Danny paused.

"Bubble gum?" he said.

The truth was, Danny had developed a full range of

gum superstitions, shifting the Kosmic Kranberry from the right side of his mouth for right-handed batters to the left side for lefties. Sticking the gum on the end of his tongue when a switch-hitter came to the plate.

"Uh, well, it's good to chew gum," Danny said, and added quickly: "But it doesn't matter what kind or anything."

"Oh, right," said Mr. Fitch, mouthing the words as he wrote them in his notepad. "Any . . . kind . . . of . . . gum."

Just as Danny was wondering if Molly's dad could possibly have any more questions, Mr. Fitch snapped his notebook shut and waved down to the front of the room where Lucas and Molly were sitting.

"Thanks, Danny, that was great," he said. "Hey, Mol, Lucas, want to see the television booth?"

Danny and Lucas looked at each other and gasped as Mr. Fitch led them to a door on the far side of the press box that had the words ON AIR lit up in red above it. He put his head around the door and they all piled in. Sitting there in front of them staring out at the field were Bullet Santana and Wally Mandelberg, the guys Danny watched on television every night.

"This is unbelievable," Lucas whispered, grabbing an extra-chunky super-fudge brownie from the food table. "Un-be-liev-able!"

Danny nodded and poked Molly in the arm.

As Santana did the play-by-play, Mandelberg turned around to shake Mr. Fitch's hand.

"Let me interrupt you there, Bullet. Folks, we've got the *Daily Bugler*'s Jim Fitch and three of his friends in the booth with us for the bottom of the ninth inning," Mandelberg said.

"I bet you kids would like to see the Sluggers win this one, huh?" said Santana, thrusting a microphone under Danny's chin.

"*Yes, sir,*" whispered Danny nervously. His voice was going out on the air! His parents and every kid he knew would be watching this. Max was probably at that very moment falling off the living room chair and convulsing on the floor in a fit of jealousy.

"Wally, Bullet, this here is Danny Gurkin, one of the biggest Sluggers fans I know. And this is my daughter, Molly Fitch, and her friend Lucas Masterly," Mr. Fitch said, leaning into the mike. "Danny's got about a million superstitions he's hoping will help the team."

"Ah, don't we all," said Bullet Santana, holding up two crossed fingers. "Well, the Sluggers could use some help. You got any ideas, kid?"

Danny was dead nervous, but looking around the booth, he did spot a couple of obvious problems.

"Well, Mr. Santana, you might want to turn your baseball cap around, especially with a righty like Tito Calagara coming to the plate," Danny said. "Uh, and I

don't want to be rude, but you should never leave two unfinished hot dogs on the table."

"There you have it, folks," Mandelberg said, picking up the two half-eaten hot dogs with a chuckle. "Well, I'm gobbling up these dogs right now."

Calagara lined a sharp single up the middle.

"Holy cow! That's a base hit," said Santana into the microphone as Molly, Lucas, and Danny cheered behind him.

"Good going, kid," said Mandelberg.

Ruffian slammed the ball into his glove and stared in at the next Sluggers batter, Bruce Minsky. Danny pressed the Kosmic Kranberry up against the roof of his mouth.

"You know, Wally, Calagara is not exactly a cheetah at first base," said Santana.

"You got that right, Bullet," Mandelberg agreed. "Watching Calagara run the bases is like trying to follow the hour hand on your wristwatch. It takes time."

As Mandelberg chewed the last bit of his second hot dog, Danny crossed his fingers and arms and stood on one leg. He cut the wad of gum in half with his tongue.

"Two pieces must be better than one," Danny thought. He closed his eyes and chewed on both sides of his mouth as Ruffian delivered.

Minsky smashed the ball through the gap in right-center field, the deepest part of the stadium.

"That's going to roll all the way to the wall!" Santana yelled. "Look at Calagara go! He's running like a man possessed. He's rounding third. . . ."

Danny opened his eyes as Tito Calagara crossed the plate with the winning run, then collapsed into the arms of his teammates. Mandelberg and Santana weren't looking at the field. They were both staring at Danny.

"We win!" Molly shouted, jumping in the air to give Lucas a double high five. "One to nothing! One to nothing!"

"You really are good luck!" gushed Mandelberg. "What did you say your name was?"

Before Danny could stutter a reply, Mr. Fitch leaned into the microphone.

"Wally, Bullet, you can read all about Danny Gurkin and his amazing superstitions in the *Daily Bugler* tomorrow. It's a must-read."

Sleepless Night

Danny stared up at the ceiling. It was two a.m., but his eyes were as big as baseballs. He still had the Kosmic Kranberry from the game in his mouth. He was too afraid to stop chewing.

Danny had spent a lifetime ordering just the right kinds of hot dogs, avoiding cracks in the sidewalk, holding his breath, and crossing every possible part of his body in an effort to help the Sluggers win.

Now finally something was working!

Danny remembered the hidden passageway in Manchester Boddlebrooks's study. He remembered the old-fashioned beakers and jars in the secret baseball-bat tower. He remembered the dusty old books on the table where he had found the gum.

The Sluggers had won every game since that night!

Something more than run-of-the-mill Gurkin superstition was at play here.

Danny reached under the bed and grabbed the three packets of gum, holding them up to the moonlight of his bedroom window. The constellations on the wrappers glittered in the blue light.

Danny stuck the wad of chewed gum under his bedside table. Then he turned over, slipped the three packets under his pillow, and drifted off to sleep, dreaming of a very large bubble-gum tycoon and his quest for the championship.

Far away in the shadows of a musty mansion, another pair of eyes was open wide, one wandering up into the moonlit night, the other squinting down at a small packet of extremely old gum.

FOURTH  INNING

The Kid Who Makes the Sluggers Win

When he got to the kitchen the next morning, Danny found a note from his mother on the table.

"Go, Sluggers! Good luck at school!" said the note. Lydia Gurkin always left the house forty-five minutes before Danny on school days because she needed time to prepare for class, and because Danny had made it clear that eleven-year-olds don't walk to school with their mothers, even if they are unfortunate enough to attend the same school where their mother teaches.

Danny's mother had waited eagerly the night before to congratulate Danny on his television debut. Harold Gurkin had been stuck at the Frompovich campaign until way past midnight, and Danny wondered if his father had even watched.

Danny heard the slap of the newspaper being delivered outside the front door and ran to pick it up. As he walked back into the kitchen with the *Daily Bugler* in hand, Danny scanned the sports page for the article by Jim Fitch.

There it was, to the left of the main story, under the headline SCHOOLBOY REVEALS AMAZING SUPERSTITION SECRETS.

Danny started reading:

BY JIM FITCH

WINNING STREAK STADIUM—Put away your lucky beads. Drop your knitting needles. Take a bath. Get to work. And for God's sake, stop translating games into Cantonese!

Superstitious Sluggers fans: your services are no longer needed.

That's because there is a boy out there who has superstition down to a science, who has more good vibes in his pinkie than all of you put together. There is a boy who roots so hard he's got all of our backs.

His name is Daniel Gurkin, he's eleven years old, and if I hadn't seen it with my own eyes, I would never have believed it. For the first time ever, the Kid Who Makes the Sluggers Win has revealed his secrets in this *Daily Bugler* exclusive.

So what are Gurkin's secrets? What does the wise one say we have to do to turn the Sluggers' nine-game winning streak into their first World Championship in 108 years?

Hot dogs. Lots of hot dogs . . .

The article said where to find Willie's cart, gave instructions for breath holding and bubble-gum chewing, and stressed the importance of avoiding cracks in the sidewalk at all costs. Mr. Fitch had remembered everything Danny told him.

The story ended:

Think the Sluggers got lucky last night? Think Tito Calagara normally runs like a gazelle that's just won the lottery, or that Bruce Minsky just happened to come through in the clutch against the most ferocious pitcher in baseball? WELL, THINK AGAIN!

It was fantastic! Danny stumbled toward the refrigerator, unable to take his eyes off the newspaper. He had never seen his name in print before, and it made the back of his neck tingle. There must have been tens of thousands of copies of the *Daily Bugler* that day, and each one had his name in it.

"Good morning, my famous son!" Danny's father said, his arms raised above his head.

Harold Gurkin was standing at the kitchen door with a grin on his face.

"Can you believe it?" Danny asked. "Did you hear me on television?"

"Of course we heard you," Harold Gurkin said. "Even the mayor heard you. I was very proud, especially when you told Wally Mandelberg to finish his hot dog! I can't believe you said that. We got about a dozen phone calls."

Danny laughed.

"Listen, I have to run, but good luck with Mrs. Sherman," his father said. He turned to go, then stopped.

"You know, Danny, I know I haven't been around much this summer, and I'm really sorry about that. I would have liked to have taken you to a few ball games and stuff like that," Danny's father said, his eyes focused on his hands. "After the campaign there'll be a lot more time."

"I understand," Danny said, even though he didn't really.

"You're a big star!" Harold Gurkin said, and a moment later he was out the door.

Danny sat at the table and read the article one more

time. There was a paper-bag lunch on the table that his mother had prepared: one egg salad sandwich, a bag of sour cream and onion potato chips, and two mushy bananas.

Danny grabbed his lunch and headed for the door. There was no putting off school any longer. As he walked out of the kitchen, a bleary-eyed Max stumbled in, in his boxer shorts and a ratty old T-shirt, clearly unconcerned by the fact he was going to be late.

"Good luck with Mrs. Sherman today," Max said. "And don't worry, she usually only eats one student on the first day, and you're too scrawny."

Danny thought about the newspaper article during the nine-block walk to school. He was still flying high when he reached the low brick box that was John J. Barnibus. The school was two stories high and about half a block long, with metal gratings over the first-floor windows and a concrete playground on the side with basketball hoops and a painted baseball diamond.

Crowds of children stood around at the front entrance. Danny scanned the crowd for Molly and Lucas, but before he could spot them somebody grabbed his arm.

"Danny! Hey, man, how was your summer?"

It was Briny Anderson, a seventh grader who was the best athlete at school. Briny was almost six feet tall, with blond hair and sunglasses. He had maybe said seven words to Danny in the three years they had been aware of each other's existence, and at least four of those words had been "huh."

"It was great, Briny," Danny replied. "Er . . . how was yours?"

"Great. Great. Great," Briny said quickly. "Listen, I was wondering if you'd consider trying out for the baseball, basketball, and tennis teams this year? Have you thought about it? We could really use you."

"Me?" Danny asked.

"Yeah," Briny continued. "You just let me know and I'll talk to the coaches and get you on the teams."

"Gosh, thanks," Danny said.

"Don't mention it," Briny said. "Anything for a friend."

Danny walked off in a daze. He'd never even thought Briny knew his name, let alone considered him a friend. He'd certainly never thought he was good enough to go out for the basketball, baseball, or tennis teams.

Danny spotted Molly and Lucas leaning against the wall near the main door. He started to walk over to them but only got about three feet before he felt an arm around his shoulder.

"Daniel Gurkin!" said a raspy voice above him. It was Principal Spinkle, the second-most-feared person at John J. Barnibus after Mrs. Sherman!

Principal Spinkle had been in charge of the school for more than forty years, and his face was marked by a deep wrinkle for each one of them, like the rings in a tree trunk.

Danny gulped.

What did the Wrinkled Spinkle want with him? Could he already be in trouble, even before a single class?

"Daniel, don't run away. I've got someone I'd like you to meet," Principal Spinkle gushed, his jowly cheeks shaking like Jell-O.

"Yes, sir," Danny said. "Sorry, sir."

Principal Spinkle had certainly never put his arm around Danny's shoulder before, and he'd never called him Daniel.

"This here is Councilman Bixby," the principal said. "He's come here to talk to us today about the importance of studying."

"Hello, Councilman Bixby," Danny said, shaking the man's hand.

"Here he is, the boy himself," Principal Spinkle said to Councilman Bixby, holding Danny by both shoulders. "You know, the one I was telling you about."

"Ohhh, right, right," said Councilman Bixby. "Well, it's an honor to meet you, son."

"Thanks," said Danny.

"We're expecting great things from Danny this year, aren't we, young man?" Principal Spinkle said, tightening his grip on Danny's shoulders.

"I guess so," said Danny.

Out of the corner of his eye, Danny could see that Molly and Lucas were staring at him, along with about half of the sixth-grade class.

"Danny, I'm sure you are aware how important it is for the students at John J. Barnibus to do well on the state aptitude exam this year," Councilman Bixby said, leaning down so that his face was level with Danny's. "There's a lot at stake — state funding, new computers — yes indeed, a lot at stake."

"I think what the councilman is saying, Danny, is that we could use all the help we can get," Principal Spinkle interjected. "Well . . . kind of like the Sluggers, see? We need the same kind of help as the Sluggers, if you catch my drift."

It was then that Danny noticed that both men were chewing bubble gum.

"Danny, I wonder if you wouldn't mind signing my *Daily Bugler*," Councilman Bixby said, thrusting out a pen and a copy of the newspaper. "It's for my kid, you understand."

Danny signed his name.

"Well, Danny, thanks again," Principal Spinkle said, patting Danny on the shoulder. Danny could swear

Principal Spinkle was trying to avoid stepping on the cracks in the sidewalk as he backed up.

"Oh, and go, Sluggers!" Principal Spinkle added, punching his fist weakly in the air.

"Yes, go, Sluggers," said Councilman Bixby.

Diamond Bob Honeysuckle IV

Diamond Bob Honeysuckle IV loved his name. He loved the power it gave him and the fear it instilled in those around him. His great-granddaddy, the original Diamond Bob, had put it to him best when he was just a small boy, knee-high to a scorpion.

"To be liked is nice," his great-granddaddy had said, slapping him lovingly across the cheek to make sure he was listening. "But it ain't worth a hill of beans."

Fear was much better for business, and business was the only thing that mattered to Diamond Bob Honeysuckle IV, the owner of the Texas Tornadoes and the master of just about everything else he laid his eyes on.

At this instant, Diamond Bob's eyes were focused on twelve exceedingly nervous men and women in business suits sitting around a long wooden table in a darkened room in the bowels of Tornado Stadium.

What little light there was in the room glinted off

the forty-seven-carat pinkie ring on Diamond Bob's right hand, which he had just slammed down on the table with the full force of a bank account that ended in ten zeroes. Underneath his hand was a copy of the *Daily Bugler*, and it was opened to the sports section.

"Who *is* this brat?" Diamond Bob demanded, pointing to the article about Danny. "And what are you people going to do about him?"

"Mr. Honeysuckle, he's just a superstitious kid who thinks he can affect the outcome of games," said one of the braver Tornado executives at the table. "He's not worth worrying about."

Diamond Bob spun around to face the man, his ten-gallon hat nearly flying off his head and a low growl emanating from his lips.

"What did you say, Bill?" he said to the man. "I must have heard you incorrectly. You couldn't possibly have said that *he's not worth worrying about*!"

"No, sir," said the man.

"It's my business to worry about everything, and don't you forget it," Diamond Bob went on. "That's why I'm the billionaire, and you're all sitting in those chairs."

"Yes, sir," the executives said in unison.

"Now, I want to keep an eye on this Gurkin kid. I want to know everything he does. What he eats for breakfast, where he goes to school, who his friends are," Diamond Bob said, wagging his finger in the air. "And

SCHOOLBOY REVEALS AMAZING
SUPERSTITION SECRETS

in the meantime, you fellas go out and find me our own lucky kid."

"Our own lucky kid?" the executive named Bill asked.

"Yes! If the Sluggers can have a lucky kid, then the Tornadoes have to have an even luckier kid," Diamond Bob shouted, a stream of spittle shooting out of his mouth.

"But, Diamond Bob, it's all made up. This Gurkin boy is just a ploy to sell newspapers," said Bill. "I mean, hot dogs and bubble gum and pencils under his nose? It's just a coincidence."

Diamond Bob stood up and slowly placed his enormous hat on the table in front of him. He would have to get some new executives, he thought, not these lily-livered college types who had no idea how the world worked.

"Gentlemen, let's get one thing clear," Diamond Bob said, pressing his knuckles down on the table until they were white. "There's no such thing as coincidence. And anything, anything at all, that makes those Sluggers believe they have a chance of beating my Tornadoes is worth worrying about, even if it is a load of hooey!"

"Yes, sir." The executives nodded.

"Now find that kid!" Diamond Bob said. "Oh, ah, and, Bill . . . you're fired."

The Snowed-Out Summer of 1934

By the time Seymour Sycamore moved into the Boddle-brooks mansion in the summer of 1934, the place had been home to three previous caretakers, men hired by Skidmore to keep an eye on the rambling estate but who had little enthusiasm for its unusual charm.

All ended up leaving in a huff, unable to cope with the mountain of rules that Manchester had laid out in his will. No going into the study. No cleaning up the popped popcorn kernels. No flying the hot-air balloon in the backyard.

Fear that the Curse of the Poisoned Pretzel might rub off on them was enough to keep the caretakers in line. But the final man couldn't resist breaking the last rule, untying the enormous bubble-shaped balloon in the dead of night and taking it out for a joyride. He floated up over West Bubble, waking the surprised residents with a terrifying laugh, then soared out over Ball Four Sound and finally drifted into the moonlit night over the Atlantic Ocean, never to be heard from again.

It had been hard to find a replacement after that, and the house lay empty for many months before Seymour Sycamore knocked on Skidmore's door.

Skidmore didn't like the new man, but he had to

admit he was taking good care of the place, and just in time too.

After decades of ineptitude, the Sluggers were suddenly playing well again. All the excitement surrounding the team's sudden rise in fortune might even make it easier to sell the ugly mansion, Skidmore thought. He might get a good price for it.

On a brilliant August morning, Skidmore's mustard yellow Rolls-Royce again pulled up outside the mansion's enormous front door. Behind him in a smaller mustard yellow car were three lawyers, two real estate agents, and the first-ever prospective buyer of the fifty-two-bedroom mansion, a chain-smoking young businessman named Erckle C. Windhammer.

The group brushed past Seymour Sycamore when he opened the hot-dog doors and immediately began sizing up the place, taking measurements of the walls, stomping on the floor to make sure it was solid, flicking the lights on and off.

"You're absolutely right, Mr. Boddlebrooks," the businessman said once they reached the grand ballroom. "It really is hideous. It'll be perfect."

"I know, I know," Skidmore chuckled. "It's a match made in heaven."

Erckle C. Windhammer was just twenty-three years old, but he had already made a fortune investing in roller coasters. He was looking for a gimmicky site to put up the world's biggest theme park, and he figured no place would be more gimmicky than Manchester Boddlebrooks's enormous bubble-gum estate.

Mr. Windhammer envisioned a mile-long roller coaster in the backyard, which he had tentatively decided to name the Monster of Manchester, and a parachute ride he was thinking of calling the Big Bad Bubble Plunge, which would be so tall it would feel like jumping out of an airplane.

The only problem was the mansion itself.

"I hope you don't mind, but I'll probably need to knock most of the building down," said Mr. Windhammer, putting out a cigarette on the floor with his shoe, then immediately reaching into his pocket for another one. "We'd just keep the facade, and maybe the ballroom, and then we'd build a haunted-house ride around it."

"Mind?" said Skidmore. "Why would I mind? That sounds like the best possible thing to do."

"I'll tell you what it sounds like," said a voice behind the two businessmen. "It sounds like a heap of baloney!"

It was Seymour Sycamore, and he was furious.

"What kind of a brother are you, sir?" said Sycamore, his good eye focused on Skidmore's nose, the other glaring straight at Windhammer, who stumbled back with fright before he recovered his composure.

The old man was chomping angrily on a piece of gum, his lips smacking together loudly.

"Don't worry, old fella," Windhammer said, sticking his finger in his neck collar to loosen it up and trying not to look Sycamore in the eye. "You can stay on and work at the haunted house. You would fit in perfectly."

"And let me remind you, Mr. Sycamore, that you aren't even really the caretaker here," Skidmore added. "This technically isn't any of your business.

"In any case," Skidmore went on, "my dear brother has been gone for more than thirty years, and there comes a time to look to the future."

"Hear, hear," said Windhammer. "Well said."

"You're making a big mistake, the both of you," warned Sycamore. "A terrible mistake."

But the theme-park entrepreneur ignored him.

"Boddlebrooks, old chap, it looks like we have a deal," he said. "Assuming, of course, that your team wins the World Series."

"Come again?" Skidmore said. "What could winning the World Series possibly have to do with it?"

"Well," Mr. Windhammer explained. "People would gladly pay to come to Manchester World Theme Park, former home of Manchester Boddlebrooks, founder of the World Champion Sluggers. But who is going to shell out for a three-hundred-pound dead guy whose team has fallen short yet again?"

"Hmm, I see your point," Skidmore said. "Well, I wouldn't worry, Mr. Windhammer. That championship is all but ours. Nothing can stand in our way now except an act of nature."

Seymour Sycamore turned on his heel and stalked toward the door, leaving Skidmore and Mr. Windhammer to stare after him. At the doorway, Sycamore paused and turned slowly toward a silver wastepaper basket. With a flourish of disgust, he spat a piece of bright red gum into the container, then slammed the door behind him.

Skidmore chuckled and patted Mr. Windhammer on the back.

"Don't mind that old fool," he said. "Business is business."

Mr. Windhammer nodded vacantly, but his eyes were fixed on the darkening clouds in the window behind Skidmore. He pulled his light jacket up tight against the cold.

"Looks like quite a storm's coming," he said.

The Two Sides of Fame

It was hard to get used to being so popular. Bobby Shrop, the brainiest guy in sixth grade, cornered Danny in science and made him swear to be his partner. Leila Markowitz and Jenny Tapanade almost knocked each other over trying to sit next to him in English class. Then Mr. Uribe pulled Danny aside at the end of Spanish.

"Un momento, por favor," Mr. Uribe said nervously. "Danny, I've been a Sluggers fan ever since my family came to this country from Peru when I was nine years old, and I don't think I can take another year of disappointment. I just wanted to let you know we're all pulling for you and hoping you'll make the difference. *Tú eres la única esperanza."*

"Gracias, Señor Uribe," Danny replied, though he wasn't entirely sure what Mr. Uribe had said. "I'll do my best."

"Imagine if they knew about the Kosmic Kranberry," Danny thought.

There was only one person who seemed to have a bad reaction to Danny's sudden fame, and it was the one person Danny was really hoping would be on his side.

"Let me make one thing crystal clear," Mrs. Sherman barked at the beginning of history class, staring straight at Danny through thick black glasses but pretending to make her remarks to the whole room. "You can eat a million hot dogs and chew a million sticks of bubble gum, but it isn't going to help you get through American history."

"Yes, ma'am," Danny, Molly, Lucas, and the

rest of the class responded in unison.

"America wasn't built by avoiding the cracks in the sidewalk!" Mrs. Sherman went on, pacing in front of her desk with her hands clasped behind her like a general. She was even wearing all green.

"I don't like baseball, and I don't like the Sluggers. What I like is hard work. Sacrifice. Commitment. In fact, I'd like a two-page essay from each of you on what hard work and sacrifice mean and how they have contributed to the history of America. I want that by tomorrow."

"Oh, man!" Danny heard himself saying.

"What's that, Mr. Gurkin?" Mrs. Sherman huffed. "Too busy talking to newspapermen to do your history homework?"

"No, ma'am," Danny said, slouching down in his chair.

"Good. Then your essay can be four pages long," Mrs. Sherman said, jerking her head up to put a quick end to the smattering of laughter that broke out behind Danny. "Anybody else have something to say?"

Nobody did.

After class, Molly and Lucas came over to console Danny on losing the first ground war against the Sherman Tank, but he had already been cornered by the Barnibus debate team and they couldn't get close.

Danny had never been the popular kid at school before. Far from it. Now he was in demand wherever he turned. He felt as if he were walking on air—other than with Mrs. Sherman, of course. Danny wondered if maybe the Wrinkled Spinkle would be willing to put in a good word with her, now that they were such close friends.

By the time Danny left John J. Barnibus, he felt as though he'd grown eight inches taller. He had walked two blocks already and said goodbye to a dozen sixth and seventh graders who wanted to talk to him about the Sluggers when he realized he had forgotten to wait for Molly and Lucas in front of school so they could all go home together.

"I'll call them later," Danny thought as he rushed home.

What he came across on the corner of Highland Avenue and Renseller Street nearly made his eyes pop out of his head. A long line of people, most with Sluggers caps on their heads and copies of the *Daily Bugler* under their arms, began at Willie's hot-dog cart and stretched as far as the eye could see.

"Get your hot dogs! Get your world-famous lucky hot dogs here!" Willie was shouting as he frantically sloshed sauerkraut and onion goop on another frank. In front of the cart, two television reporters were peppering Willie with questions. He was doing his best to answer them while his hands kept pace with hot-dog demand.

"The full name is William de la Bosque de Monte-carlo, but people just call me Willie," he said. "Yeah, I've been involved in the culinary industry for fourteen years. . . . Oh, yes, always as a hot-dog man.

"How long have I known Danny Gurkin? Well, let's see . . . ages, I guess. He *is* one lucky kid. Two hot dogs before every game. That's exactly right."

Danny was about to cross the street when he noticed a long black car driving slowly up the other side of the street. It had a diamond-studded hood ornament that glinted in the sun like a prism.

He glanced at the license plate: DB-IV.

Danny had a strange feeling that the car had been behind him for a while. Was the same black car outside school when he left? Danny tried to think back, but he'd run out in such a hurry he couldn't remember.

Inside the car were two men in expensive-looking suits and clip-on sunglasses. They were staring straight ahead at the road, but Danny had the sense they had been looking at him just a minute before. The driver was big and round with meaty red hands, and the man in the passenger seat had a pasty face and a dark goatee.

As Danny looked over, the two men quickly turned their heads away.

Was it his imagination? There was only one way to find out.

Danny turned around and hopped back on the curb, pulling his Sluggers cap low over his eyes. He hustled back down Highland Avenue and glanced over his shoulder as casually as he could. The car had turned around and was about half a block behind him.

"Who are they?" Danny wondered. The men looked too rich to be reporters.

When Danny finally got to Chorloff Street, he broke into a run, then scurried up the front stoop and up the stairs to his apartment.

He dropped his backpack on the living room floor, then ran over to the window. The black car was parked on the corner just across the street from Danny's house, and the two men were sitting in the front seat munching on what appeared to be tacos.

Thump!

The front door of the apartment slammed shut, and Danny practically jumped out of his skin. He shot away from the window and crouched down behind the television.

"What are you doing behind the television?" Max said, glancing over at Danny with amusement.

"Behind the television?" Danny replied. "Oh, I just dropped something."

"It looks like you're hiding down there," Max said. "What's the problem? All this fame going to your head?"

"You heard about the newspaper article?" Danny asked, standing up as nonchalantly as he could.

"Heard about it? How could I not?" said Max. "Everyone at Canfield has heard about it. I spent all day explaining about my weird superstitious brother."

"Really?" said Danny.

"At least you're good for something, though," Max went on, plopping down on the living room chair and fishing his headphones out of his jacket. "I got a date with Sarah McAllister out of it, which isn't too shabby. She's been ignoring me since I was your age."

That was—almost—the first nice thing Max had said to Danny in about three years.

"Hey, Max," Danny asked nervously. "I was wondering, did you notice that black car parked outside?"

"Nope," said Max, sticking the earphones into his ears.

Danny hesitated, but he had to say something.

"Max, I think somebody might be following me," Danny said. "That's why I, uh, was behind the television."

"Who would want to follow you?" his brother laughed.

"I don't know, but they're still parked outside," Danny replied. "Just down the street. You can see them from the window."

"No way!" said Max, getting up and moving over to the window. "Where?"

Danny pointed toward the spot where the car had been, but it was gone. The only evidence that the men had been there at all was a discarded taco box lying on its side against the curb, next to two crumpled-up copies of the *Daily Bugler*.

The Search for the Lucky Kid

The state of Texas awoke the following Thursday to a call to arms. From the scorched plains of the Panhandle to the prairies of the northeast, a mysterious poster suddenly appeared. Written in the old style of the Wild West and signed by Diamond Bob Honeysuckle IV himself, it said simply:

WANTED: ONE LUCKY KID

His Tornadoes had lost the final two games of the series to the Sluggers, but Diamond Bob was not concerned. He was certain his executives would soon find him the luckiest kid money could buy. He would not spare any expense in the search. Overnight, an army of blue-haired secretaries was assembled to man the phone banks in a glass-walled conference room overlooking Tornado Field.

The oil magnate paced back and forth in his luxurious office, his ten-gallon hat in his hands, and waited for news of the calls flooding in from downstairs.

At ten a.m., Diamond Bob couldn't take it anymore. He adjusted his solid-silver belt buckle, pulled his hat down over his eyes, and marched down to the conference room to see what was going on.

There was a quick shuffling as the telephone operators stashed away their magazines and nail files when the tycoon swung into the room. Other than that, there was quiet.

The posters had reached every corner of the Lone Star State, but it was hard to motivate fans who had known nothing but a century of success, people who had never before been asked to do anything for their team but purchase overpriced nachos at the concession stand.

"What in blazes is going on?" Diamond Bob screamed at his personal assistant, Wallace, who was already cowering against the wall in anticipation of just such an outburst. "The only things ringing in here are your hands!"

"Uh, sir, that would be 'wringing,' with a *w*," said Wallace.

Diamond Bob glared at Wallace in a way that made

it clear he should be looking for a new job. He shifted his weight from one double-stitched alligator-skin cowboy boot to the other.

Finally, a phone rang at a desk in the back of the room.

Diamond Bob and his staff ran over and stood behind the poor telephone operator as she answered the call.

"Yes, this is Tornadoes headquarters," the operator said.

"Yes, we are looking for a lucky kid, that's exactly right," she went on, glancing nervously over her shoulder at the executives behind her.

"Yes, we want someone who really loves the Tornadoes," she gushed. "But are you lucky?

"Hmm, hmm, right. Well, I'd have to ask, but I'd say that being extremely rich is a good sign that you are lucky," she said, turning to Diamond Bob, who nodded his approval.

"Yes. Yes. Yes," chirped the operator. This sounded promising! Perhaps they had their lucky kid. A Tornadoes' Danny Gurkin.

"There could be big money in that," Diamond Bob thought. He imagined a line of Tornado Kid action figures, maybe even a new kind of gasoline that he could sell at a premium. Lucky Unleaded, or Fortuitous Fuel. He liked the sound of that.

But suddenly the operator's smile fell away.

"No," she said dejectedly. "No, sir, you can't have the job if you are forty-seven. No, you have to be a child, sir. I'm sorry."

Diamond Bob turned and kicked the wall with his cowboy boot.

Danny in Demand

"That's *H-O-R*," Lucas gloated as Danny's shot clanked off the rim. He grabbed the ball and passed it on a bounce to Molly. "You might be the most famous eleven-year-old in the world, Danny, but you still suck at horse!"

Molly grabbed the ball and dribbled over to the side of the basket.

"Underhand. Eyes closed. Off the backboard," she said, before swishing in the shot. "Beat that, Hot Dog Boy!"

It was Saturday morning at Quincy Park, and they all had survived the first week of school.

The park was packed with kids, each of them with one eye on the games they were playing and the other on Danny Gurkin. Danny had expected the attention to fade away, but it only grew with each Sluggers victory.

Wherever Danny went, people stopped and shook his hand. Grown men asked for his autograph; teenage girls giggled at his approach. At hospitals around the city, at least three newborn babies had been named Gurkin in his honor. It was surreal.

The Sluggers lost only once all week, when Mrs. Sherman ordered Danny to take the Kosmic Kranberry out of his mouth during a Friday-afternoon game against the Baltimore Bobcats. Danny wasn't sure if chewing the gum would work if he wasn't watching the game on TV or listening to the radio, but he figured he'd give it a shot.

"Is that *bubble gum* I smell?" said Mrs. Sherman, spinning around to face the class, then slowly making her way down the row of desks until she got to Danny's. It wasn't hard to find the culprit because the Kosmic Kranberry smelled so bad.

"Mr. Gurkin! I should have known," Mrs. Sherman said with a sneer, extending a khaki glove and gesturing for Danny to hand over the gum. Danny panicked and swallowed it instead, earning an hour's detention and a two-page essay assignment on the importance that respecting one's elders had played in the history of the United States of America.

With a dozen games left in the season, the Sluggers were now just six games behind the Tornadoes, and only three behind the Oakland Ogres for the wild-card spot.

They had passed seven other teams in the standings since their winning streak began.

Danny had not seen the black car or its passengers since the first day of school, but he kept finding clues that the men might still be around. One morning he spotted a half-eaten burrito on his stoop, and another day a crumpled-up paper bag from the House of Tacos blew by him on the street in front of school.

"I must be imagining all this," Danny thought.

He had other worries as well, particularly what to do about his dwindling supply of Kosmic Kranberry. He had just eight sticks left, nowhere near enough for the rest of the season and the play-offs, if the Sluggers could make it that far.

"Your shot, Danny," Molly said, snapping her fingers in front of Danny's face. "Earth to Hot Dog Boy."

"Sorry," Danny said. "What's the score?"

"You're losing," said Lucas. "That's all you need to know."

Danny lined up a shot from the foul line but missed badly, the ball clanking off the rim and ricocheting straight down at the ground.

"Man, you're awful today," Lucas said.

"I know," Danny replied meekly.

Between his sudden fame, the mysterious black car, and the burden of keeping the biggest secret of his life, Danny couldn't concentrate on basketball.

Three times that week he had picked up the phone to tell Molly and Lucas about the Kosmic Kranberry, and three times he had hung up. He'd almost told them after his run-in with Mrs. Sherman in history class, but he'd been sidetracked by a crush of new friends and hangers-on and forgotten all about them.

Now Danny was on the verge of spilling the beans again, but something held him back.

"Hey, you guys haven't noticed a black car around school with these two guys inside?" Danny said instead.

"Maybe," said Molly. "There are a lot of black cars."

"Yeah, but this one has a sparkly hood ornament that looks like it's made out of diamonds, and a weird license plate, DB-IV."

"DB-IV?" said Molly. "What could that stand for?"

"I don't know," said Danny. "I think it's following me."

Just then, Briny Anderson sauntered over from the seventh graders' court, casually spinning a basketball on his index finger as if it were the easiest thing in the world to do.

"Hey, Danny, my man!" Briny said, giving him a high five, then holding his palm out behind his back to receive one from Danny. "How you doin'?"

"Oh, I'm cool, Briny," Danny said. "Just shooting some hoops, you know."

"Yeah, right," Briny said, nodding at Molly and

Lucas. "Hey, Mandy, Louis, how you doin'?"

"Uh, it's Molly and Lucas," Danny said.

"Oh, yeah, yeah, right," said Briny. "Listen, Danny, the guys on the baseball team are having a little party tonight at my place and we were wondering if you wanted to come. It's mostly just for the starting players actually, but we decided to invite you too, seeing as you might be trying out for the team. We're serving hot dogs."

"Wow," said Danny. "That'd be great. Can I bring my friends?"

Briny glanced over at the others.

"Well . . . it's really just for the team, actually," he said slowly.

"Oh," said Danny. "Right."

Molly was staring at them with her eyes narrowed like a cat's. Lucas's smile had quickly turned to a scowl.

"Anyway, I'll see you there," Briny went on, giving Danny another high five, this one with his elbow.

"So long, Marnie, Leroy," he called back as he walked away.

Mayor Fred Frompovich Gets an Idea

If there was one thing Mayor Fred Frompovich knew, it was how to win an election. You had to have vision. You had to have strategy. You had to have compassion.

None of those things, however, was as valuable as a superstitious eleven-year-old who had captured the public's attention.

"I'm not asking for the moon, Harold. I just want fifteen minutes with your son," the mayor said, leaning against the mahogany desk in his office at City Hall and beaming at Harold Gurkin. He had his shirtsleeves rolled up and his black suit jacket draped over his chair. The office had the distinct smell of cigarette smoke, but Harold Gurkin figured it was better not to go into that with the mayor, who had sworn he was going to quit following the spontaneous combustion fiasco.

"Maybe we could be photographed together at a Sluggers game. Yes, that would be ideal," said the mayor.

Harold Gurkin was sitting in a plush leather armchair in front of the mayor's desk, fiddling nervously with a pencil. He was stalling for time.

"I don't know, Mr. Mayor. I'd have to talk to my wife, and ask Danny if he even wanted to do something like that," he said. "That's a lot of attention for a kid to deal with."

The mayor pressed a button on his intercom and called through to his secretary.

"Margaret, can you get us two cigars? The Cuban ones I save for special occasions," he purred, and then turned his gaze back to Harold Gurkin.

"Don't think I don't understand your reservations, Harry," the mayor said, though the look of determination on his face made it clear that Harold Gurkin's reservations were not his primary concern. "But as my campaign manager, you have to admit we need that lucky kid of yours. The whole election might depend on it!"

Harold Gurkin had to agree. It would probably help, and Danny would be excited to do it. But he grimaced at the prospect of telling Lydia. She was already tired of the campaign, and this would not go over well.

"I'll ask," Mr. Gurkin told the mayor.

"That's great, Harry. Thanks a million." The mayor grinned.

The Gurkin Report

Diamond Bob sat alone at the head of his conference table and stared down at the leather-bound report in front of him. This is what he had been waiting for from his high-priced spies for two long weeks, even as his own lucky-kid search had proven an utter failure.

Diamond Bob was nervous as he ran his fingers over the gold embossed lettering on the front cover:

GURKIN REPORT, TOP-SECRET

The oil tycoon took a deep breath, then flipped the report open and began to read. What he found was truly disturbing.

The document was laid out like a traditional scouting report from one of the Tornadoes' fleet of talent scouts, but instead of sections on batting, throwing, and baserunning, it was broken down into categories like dedication, innovation, and luck.

Diamond Bob had never seen anything like it. Danny's scores for every category were off the charts. Diamond Bob bit down on his thumbnail as he came to the conclusion:

"We are dealing with a boy who can name the favorite toothpaste of every player on the team and who has a different superstition for each of them. A child who never misses a pitch, whose unwavering belief in his awful team is infectious. Someone who lives and breathes baseball. In short, a fanatic," it read. "A talent like this comes around once in a generation, perhaps once a century. In our opinion, the Tornadoes have two choices: buy every hot dog in North America, or sign the Gurkin kid up immediately . . . and at whatever the cost."

Diamond Bob scowled into the darkness of the empty room. It didn't seem possible.

The billionaire pressed a button on the intercom:

"Truffaut, Hickock, get in here," he said.

A moment later, Calamity Truffaut, the larger of the two men, and Mortimer Hickock, who bore an unfortunate resemblance to a ferret, strode into the room. They had been summoned back to Texas just for this meeting and were booked on a flight leaving an hour later to get right back on the Gurkin case. The men had been working for Diamond Bob for years, but this was the first time they had been called on to judge the skills of an eleven-year-old.

"Are you telling me he hasn't stepped on a single crack in the sidewalk the entire time you've been watching him?" Diamond Bob asked incredulously.

"Not one," Truffaut insisted.

"He can hold a pencil under his nose for three straight innings?" Diamond Bob marveled.

"I'm afraid it's true, sir," Truffaut replied. "We've got pictures."

"And the hot dogs . . . ?" said the oil tycoon, glancing down at the pages and waving his hands in disbelief.

"Before every single game," Hickock piped up. "I've never seen anything like it, boss. Frankly, he frightens me."

This was not at all what Diamond Bob wanted to hear.

But other than a few burrito stains on some of the

inside pages, it was a flawless bit of scouting, the kind that had kept the Texas Tornadoes in front of teams like the Sluggers for decades. Diamond Bob slammed the report down on the table and picked up the phone.

It was time to break the bank.

FIFTH INNING

Danny Strikes Out

Danny stood in the batter's box and concentrated as hard as he could on the pitch from Briny Anderson. He swung softly, just to make contact, but the ball whistled past his bat and crashed into the metal fence behind. It was the tenth time in a row that had happened.

"What's the problem, Danny?" Briny shouted from the dirt patch that served as a mound at the ball field at Quincy Park. "I'm just tossing it in there so you can hit it. There's nothing on these pitches at all."

Baseball season didn't start at John J. Barnibus until the spring, but Briny figured it would be good to get Danny some practice in early, seeing as he wasn't exactly famous around the neighborhood for his athletic ability. Briny only wanted him on the team as a good-luck charm, but school rules meant every player had to bat at least one time each game. Danny was definitely going to need some help.

Danny and Briny had been practicing for more than an hour, and things weren't going very well.

"Sorry, Briny," Danny said, slamming the bat into his sneaker in frustration. "Throw me one more."

"All right," Briny said. "But you've got to concentrate. Be the ball!"

Briny went into his windup and released again, the baseball shooting out of his hand much faster than Danny thought possible.

"Just make contact! Just make contact!" Danny thought as he swung, eyes focused on the white blur coming toward him.

Whiff!

The ball slammed into the backstop again. Danny's body was twisted around, the bat behind his left shoulder and his legs jutting out in awkward directions.

As he spun around, Danny noticed two figures leaning against the screen behind him. It was Molly and Lucas.

"Hey, guys. You want to play?" He smiled. "I kind of suck at this."

Molly and Lucas looked at each other, then turned

back to Danny, who was busy looking for the ball.

"Maybe another time," Molly said.

"Yeah, we're meeting the Triptiki twins for a game of two-on-two," Lucas added, kicking the dirt at his feet.

"Oh," said Danny. "That's cool."

"Throw the ball back already," Briny shouted. "You're hopeless, man!"

As Danny picked up the ball, Molly and Lucas turned on their heels and walked off toward the courts. Danny stood and stared after them until he had to get into position for the pitch.

This time Briny flung the ball even faster, and Danny didn't even have time to get his bat off his shoulder before he heard it clank into the screen.

"Hey, Danny, let's call it a day," Briny said impatiently. "You couldn't hit water if I threw you off a boat!"

Briny ran over to give Danny a high five. Then he picked up his gear and sloped off with a backward wave, leaving Danny standing alone in the batter's box.

A Flash of Fame

Mayor Fred Frompovich reached down and grabbed Danny's hand in his big, clammy fist, a dozen camera flashes going off as he did. The mayor kept his hands well manicured for occasions just such as these, and he topped off the effect with a smile that said "I like you" and "I'm in charge" at the same time.

"The Sluggers' two biggest fans, together just in time for the team's biggest game!" the mayor gushed, his eyes twinkling at the cameras as he gripped Danny's hand. They were standing on the street in front of City Hall, beside a silver limousine that had pulled up to take Danny and the mayor to Winning Streak Stadium.

It was a big night.

With just four games left in the season, the Sluggers could clinch a wild-card spot and the team's first play-off appearance in 108 years if they beat the Oakland Ogres. Frompovich had waited until this game for his photo op with Danny because his strategists told him everyone in town would be watching, and he'd be more likely to get a bump in the polls.

Inside the limousine, Harold Gurkin rubbed his forehead. It had taken him days to get the courage up to ask his wife about the mayor's campaign idea, and when he finally did, she hadn't liked it one bit.

"It's bad enough that we've lost you to that blasted campaign, Harold," she said. "Now you want to get Danny mixed up in all of this? He's only eleven years old!"

"But, sweetie, it won't be anything like that," Harold pleaded.

"That guy is such a phony," Lydia said. "I wouldn't even vote for him myself if he weren't your boss."

"Look, Lydia, I'm under a bit of pressure here," Harold snapped. "We're neck and neck in the polls, and we really need to win this one. Frompovich is the only guy with a real plan to move the city forward. I can't believe I'm saying this, but Danny's a hot commodity right now. He might really help the campaign."

"He's not a commodity, Harold," Lydia shot back. "He's your son."

"Oh, you know exactly what I mean," Danny's father replied. "It's just one night. It's not like I'm asking for the moon."

"It's your conscience," Lydia said.

"It's my job too," Harold mumbled.

The City Hall handshakes finished, the mayor and Danny joined Danny's father in the back of the limousine. It was the first time Danny had ever been in such a fancy car, and he looked around in amazement. The limo had a stereo and a bar and a small table in the middle with peanuts and potato chips laid out on it.

"Cool!" Danny said.

The minute the doors closed and the news cameras were out of sight, Mayor Frompovich reached into his jacket pocket and fished out a pack of Machismo cigarettes. He deftly tapped the pack against his knee so that just one cigarette popped out, then pulled it out the rest of the way with his teeth.

"You got yourself one heck of a good kid here, Harry," the mayor said, lighting the cigarette and taking a long drag. "One heck of a good kid."

The mayor put a hand on Danny's shoulder and fixed a million-dollar smile on Harold Gurkin.

"We might even have a spot for him in the administration after we win in November. Honorary commissioner of good fortune or something like that," Frompovich said.

"I think Danny will probably be too busy with the sixth grade for that, Mr. Mayor," Harold said quickly. "But it's very kind of you to offer."

As the limousine screeched down the concrete driveway to a VIP parking lot under Winning Streak Stadium, the mayor turned to Danny.

"So how does it work, this luck thing?" he said, and by the look on his face, it seemed as if he really wanted to know.

"Well, Mr. Mayor—" Danny began, but the mayor cut him off.

"Call me Freddie," he said.

"Mr. Mayor, really!" Harold protested, but Frompovich dismissed him with a wave of his hand.

"Well, ah, Freddie," Danny began slowly, glancing

over at his dad. "You just have to want your team to win more than anything else in the world, and then do what your heart tells you. Hold your breath. Eat a hot dog. Whatever."

"Fascinating," said Frompovich, blowing a series of smoke rings into the air.

"A stash of magic gum doesn't hurt either," Danny thought with a smile. The thought gave him an idea.

"You know, Mr. Mayor—uh, I mean, Freddie," Danny began. "There is one thing you could do that would be very good luck. It might even help you get elected."

Elected!

The mere mention of the word made Mayor Frompovich's ears prick up.

"I'm sorry, Mr. Mayor," Harold Gurkin said sternly, nudging Danny's foot. "My son sometimes gets a little ahead of himself and doesn't know his place. Danny, this is the mayor. He knows just how to get elected."

"No, Harold," Fred Frompovich said, flicking the rest of the cigarette out the window and leaning in toward Danny. "Let the boy talk."

Harold Gurkin slouched down in his seat.

"Well, Freddie," Danny said, leaning in himself and putting his arm on the mayor's shoulder. "How would you like to go down in history as the man who saved the Boddlebrooks mansion?"

The Fall of Skidmore Boddlebrooks

The Sluggers did not win the pennant in 1934, of course. Nobody did.

The snow that started falling in August did not let up until the following March, and by then the season had been canceled, along with Halloween, Thanksgiving, Christmas, and New Year's Eve.

It was too cold to celebrate.

Erckle C. Windhammer never came back to West Bubble to build his theme park. What would have been the point?

Of even more concern to Skidmore Boddlebrooks, the cold spell had nearly put his Twisty-Doughy Pretzel Company out of business. None of the employees could make it in to work through the twenty-foot-high snowdrifts that had turned West and East Bubble into an arctic tundra, and it wouldn't have made any difference if they had. The pretzel machines were too cold to handle, and the dough shattered in your hands when you touched it.

The Ball-Park Mustard Goo factory lay idle too. Had

there been a market for extra-spicy mustard snow cones, Skidmore Boddlebrooks would have had it cornered, but none existed.

Each week, the bank sent a brave courier to dig through the snow to Skidmore's East Bubble mansion with a sealed envelope that held a card showing his bank-account balance. And with each week, the number got lower and lower. Finally, it was so easy to remember that the courier stopped carrying a letter and simply told Skidmore how much money was left.

The final knock on the door came shortly before Christmas. Skidmore's mansion still looked grand from the outside, but inside it was empty. Most of the furniture had been sold off or burned as firewood, and Skidmore had taken to sleeping on a small cot.

It was late in the afternoon by the time the bank courier arrived, but Skidmore greeted his visitor unshaven and in his mustard yellow pajamas.

"Hey, you got twenty-three dollars and thirteen cents in the bank," the courier mumbled from behind a thick wool scarf that covered his mouth and most of his face. He was bundled up in a sheepskin jacket, earmuffs, mittens, two pairs of pants, and an enormous fur hat, and he was stomping up and down on a pair of wooden snowshoes to stay warm.

Back in late August, the bank man had addressed

Skidmore as "Mr. Boddlebrooks, sir." But as the mustard millionaire's savings dwindled, his greeting had changed to simply "Hey, you!" Knowing the man had only $23.13 in the bank, the courier felt no compulsion to honor Skidmore with any title at all.

"Perhaps the bank could see its way clear to extend me a small loan, just until the spring," Skidmore said, scratching his head with one hand and clutching a stale pretzel in the other.

"Fat chance. This place is already mortgaged to the hilt," said the bank man. "Oh, and Boddlebrooks, I won't be trekking back here again next week.

"In fact, I imagine you'll soon be hearing from our lawyers," he added, turning his back on Skidmore and climbing up the white mountain of snow from which he had come. "Assuming we can find any lawyers in this weather, that is."

The Roar of the Crowd

Danny spun around in wonder on the grass behind home plate, blinking up into the glare of the stadium lights. The crowd was enormous, a wall of clapping little dots that rose into the upper decks.

They were all cheering for him.

Flashbulbs burst from every corner of the stadium

like fireflies in an immense field. The stadium public-address system was so loud it shook Danny's eardrums. It took him a second to realize it was blaring the theme song from *Superman*.

"Come on, kid!" Mayor Frompovich shouted, nudging Danny from behind. "It's time to make some news."

As they walked toward the mound, Danny looked out at the giant-screen TV behind the center field wall.

His jaw dropped.

The television was showing a cartoon of a boy that looked remarkably like him swooping in on a cape, a hot dog firmly clutched in his right hand. The words HOT-DOG HERO! flashed on the bottom of the screen, and the crowd cheered even louder.

Suddenly, a man in a metal mask with a lobster red chest protector strode toward him from the Sluggers' dugout. He was enormous, like a redwood tree with legs.

"Kid, I've been wanting to meet you," said the man, thrusting an official big-league baseball into Danny's hand.

Danny gasped as the man pushed back his mask. It was Chico Medley, the Sluggers' catcher, and he was trailed by Chuck Sidewinder, Boom-Boom Bigersley, and Sid Canova. They all looked so much bigger than on television.

"You, uh, you have?" Danny said, gripping the ball with both hands, his fingers rubbing the curved red seams.

"Hey, my friend," said Sidewinder, holding out his fist for Danny to tap. "You're good luck!"

"Could you kiss my bat?" asked Bigersley, bending down and holding out his thirty-eight-ounce Louisville Slugger. "I'm in a bit of a slump."

Sid Canova gave Danny a high five.

"I'm not going to wash that hand for a week," the rookie pitcher said.

"Me neither," said Danny.

Mayor Frompovich was already standing behind a microphone set up next to the pitching mound, waving his arms above his head.

"How about a big hand for my close friend Danny Gurkin!" boomed the mayor, gesturing for Danny to join him.

With Danny at his side, the mayor shushed the crowd and began to speak, his wide, sympathetic eyes slowly scanning the stands, trying to make contact with all fifty-five thousand fans.

"For one hundred and eight long years, this city has been waiting for a night like tonight, waiting to get back to the play-offs," Frompovich began, his voice echoing through the stadium. "For one hundred and eight long years, we and our forefathers have brought our hopes and dreams to this field, and we have left it with only one thing."

The mayor shook his head sadly.

"That's right, people, I'm talking about pain," the mayor said.

"A century of pain. Five score and eight years of pain. According to my office assistant, who figured it out on his computer this morning, we're talking about nearly *fifty-seven million minutes* of pain."

The crowd sat and contemplated what a long, hard wait it had been.

"If pain could be harnessed into power, none of us in this city would get electricity bills," Frompovich went on.

The mayor raised his fist in the air defiantly.

"Well, my friends, somebody *has* turned that pain into power. Somebody standing right next to me. A boy named Danny Gurkin."

The PA system cranked up again, and the crowd began to cheer. Mayor Frompovich milked the moment for everything he could.

"I don't want to hold up the game," the mayor went on. "But I do have one important announcement to make.

"Just five minutes ago, I placed an urgent call to my dear friend Clyde Ramrod, the chairman of the West Bubble Town Council," the mayor said. "Ladies and

gentlemen, I put it to him straight in a way my opponent never would, and Mr. Ramrod has given me his word.

"He says to tell you that plans to demolish

Manchester Boddlebrooks's bubble-gum mansion have been scrapped! In fact, he has promised to start renovations immediately, and it will reopen to the public soon. That building will stand forever as a monument to our delivery from pain!" Frompovich shouted, his voice echoing through the stadium.

The crowd began to murmur. People nodded as they realized what the mayor was talking about. Most had only been faintly aware the bubble-gum building still existed, and even fewer knew it was about to be demolished.

A few fans began to clap. In moments, the entire stadium was on its feet.

Danny looked at the mayor quizzically. Five minutes earlier, Frompovich had been smoking a cigarette in the back of his limousine. When had he had a chance to call Clyde Ramrod, whoever that was, and get him to promise not to tear down the mansion?

It was time for Danny to deliver the first pitch and his palms were sweating. Chico Medley squatted down behind home plate and held out his mitt.

"Whatever you do, don't bounce the ball!" Danny told himself.

Danny put his foot on the pitching rubber and went into a windup.

Zing!

The ball zipped into Medley's mitt as straight as a dart, a strike down the middle of the plate!

"Nice toss, kid," Medley said, running out to the mound to return the ball to Danny. "You make sure and stay on our side!"

The crowd cheered as Danny held up the ball and waved. He was starting to like this fame thing.

"Now enjoy the game, everybody," the mayor shouted. "And make sure to vote come November!"

As Danny and the mayor walked off the field, Fred Frompovich held Danny's hand in his own like a prize-fighter's.

"Don't worry, kid," the mayor muttered through his teeth. "We'll call Clyde later. He owes me a couple of favors."

A Date with Destiny

If you hadn't been part of the suffering, you couldn't possibly have understood how it felt when the last pitch from Sid Canova flew past Ogres shortstop A. A. Perisho, clinching a 4–2 victory and the Sluggers first post-season appearance since early man began walking upright.

Well, practically that long.

Older fans looked to the skies, half expecting the snow to begin falling again. Many simply stared in disbelief. Some cried. Others danced into the wee hours.

Nobody who was alive remembered the Sluggers' first championship year, and many had gone to meet their maker without ever tasting the sweetness of a night like this.

But even death couldn't stop the celebration. Sluggers faithful shared the news of the team's play-off spot with loved ones in the hereafter, trekking to cemeteries across town to place copies of the *Daily Bugler* atop the tombs of those who had passed on.

The dead and the living alike took great pleasure in Jim Fitch's article in the morning edition:

BY JIM FITCH

WINNING STREAK STADIUM—The century that wouldn't end is over. After 108 long years, the Sluggers are in the play-offs. Let me write that again for those of you who still don't believe it.

The Sluggers are in the play-offs!

Try jotting that down on a notepad at home, or scribble it on the back of your hand, or stamp it with pride on your neighbor's forehead. If you write it enough times, you just might believe it.

Usually, sportswriters tell you about what has already happened, but unless you are living in a cave or have just returned from outer space, it's a pretty safe bet you already know about every single pitch that was thrown last night.

So instead, let me make a prediction: the Sluggers have a Date with Destiny.

Yes, there is the small matter of our best-of-five series against the Charleston Bruisers.

Puh-*leeze!*

And of course, the Tornadoes still have to annihilate the Minnesota Muckrakers.

Yawn.

But, my friends, make no mistake. The inevitable is hurtling toward us like an asteroid on a collision course with Earth.

The fight for the pennant will soon be upon us.

Sluggers vs. Tornadoes. Grit vs. Greed. Good vs. Evil.

Somewhere out there, somewhere *up* there, a very large bubble-gum tycoon is smiling.

Never before had a newspaper article proved so prophetic. The Sluggers and the Tornadoes raced through the first round of the play-offs as if they were late for a movie. The Tornadoes beat Minnesota 7–0, 11–1, and 17–3, so humiliating the Muckrakers that the team considered moving to Florida and joining a senior citizens' softball league.

The victory was little comfort to Diamond Bob Honeysuckle IV, who barely watched a single pitch.

Like a king who had seen an oracle foretelling his downfall, he had become obsessed with Danny Gurkin. The boy was the first thing Diamond Bob thought about when he woke up in the morning and the last thing plaguing him when he went to bed each night.

More than anything, his mind raced back to an interview he'd done during spring training in which he'd vowed that if the woeful Sluggers ever made the play-offs, his team would merrily give up home-field advantage against them, and he would eat a heaping helping of super-hot Texas chili, right out of his beloved ten-gallon hat.

Why, oh why, had he been so boastful? Diamond Bob thought.

On the evening that the Sluggers completed their own first-round play-off sweep, crushing the Bruisers 14–4 behind the inspired pitching of Vince Spagu and some pretty nifty bubble-gum chewing by Danny, Diamond Bob awoke with a start. The oil tycoon's forehead was wet with perspiration and his eyes wide with fright.

He sat up in bed, and his mind flashed back across the decades to a warning his great-grandfather had given him from his hospital bed, when Diamond Bob was still just a boy.

"If you remember just one thing I tell you about life, let it be this," his great-grandfather had said, his long, wrinkled fingers grabbing hold of young Diamond Bob's shirt. "When you've got a man down, you don't let him get up. You understand that, son?"

"Not really, Great-granddaddy. What man do you mean?" the young Diamond Bob asked. His great-grandfather might have been near death, but he still had the strength to yank the young boy toward him.

"Boy, don't you *ever* let them Sluggers get up!" his great-grandfather wheezed through a fit of coughing. "The second they get up, they'll get hope. And the second they get hope, we're in trouble."

"Why do we hate the Sluggers so much?" the young Diamond Bob asked.

This time his great-grandfather's coughing got even worse—so bad, in fact, that a team of doctors rushed in to see what was the matter.

"Them Sluggers are cursed!" the old man hissed, his eyes bulging out of his head. "Lose to a cursed team and the curse will fall on you."

Diamond Bob Honeysuckle IV scrunched up his bedcovers as he recollected the scene.

Then he picked up the phone.

"Truffaut. Wake up! And get Hickock up too," he shouted. "I'm coming out there at once. I want to meet that kid."

Molly Suspects

Molly Fitch was not a superstitious sort of girl. She had suggested her father do a story on Danny all those weeks before because she knew how crazy her friend was about eating hot dogs and crossing his fingers and toes, but she was far too practical to think that any of that stuff actually worked.

After all, Danny had been eating hot dogs and closing windows and encouraging his mother to do the dishes during games for as long as Molly could remember, but the Sluggers still always used to lose.

Not anymore.

Everything had changed, both in Danny and the once-hapless Sluggers, since they made their amazing trip out to the Boddlebrooks mansion, and it seemed impossible to chalk the transformation up entirely to coincidence.

Molly had replayed the adventure in her mind about a thousand times: the scary Mr. Sycamore, the hot-dog doors and the popcorn-popping room, the smelly bedroom made of sauerkraut. It was all so strange.

But one image stuck in her head more than any other.

It was the look on Danny's face as he rushed up to her, Lucas, and Mr. Sycamore in the grand hallway after escaping from Boddlebrooks's study. His cheeks were flushed and his eyes were darting from side to side almost as fast as Mr. Sycamore's.

He looked as if he had seen . . . not a ghost, really, but something as weird as a ghost.

"Where have you been?" the old man had asked sharply, pounding his cane on the floor.

"Sorry, Mr. Sycamore. I had to run to the bathroom," Danny had said quickly. "I guess it was that popcorn I ate before you warned me about it."

The old man had huffed and looked Danny up and down, but he didn't challenge him.

There had definitely been something odd about Danny's behavior, Molly thought as she recollected the scene. He had avoided Mr. Sycamore's gaze, which was to be expected. But he hadn't looked Molly or Lucas in the eye either. Plus, Danny had kept his right hand in his pocket the entire time and wouldn't take it out even to shake Mr. Sycamore's hand when they left.

When they got to their bikes, Molly had meant to ask Danny about what he had seen, but in the rush to get home, she hadn't had a chance. Later, she figured Danny would tell her about it, but he never spoke of the study again.

As she walked home from school with Lucas the day after the Sluggers won their first-round play-off series — after their famous friend had yet again forgotten to meet up with them after school — Molly finally put into words what had been troubling her all along.

"Why do you think Danny's never mentioned what happened in the study?" she asked, biting her thumbnail nervously.

"What study? You mean the one out at the mansion?" Lucas replied, and shrugged. "Who knows? Maybe it just wasn't very interesting."

"Come on, Lucas!" said Molly. "How could it not be interesting? Don't you remember how mad Mr. Sycamore got when Danny just put his hand on the doorknob?"

"I guess you're right," Lucas said.

"And another thing I don't understand," Molly began as they stepped down off the curb at the end of Wyatt Avenue. "How in the world did the old man not catch him?"

"That's a good question," Lucas said. "Danny must have hidden somewhere really good. Yeah, you'd think he would have been bragging about that for weeks."

Lucas kicked a crumpled newspaper that was lying in the street.

"Then there's the whole business of the black car he said was following him," Molly said. "That was pretty weird too, huh?"

"Yeah. It is odd," Lucas conceded.

They walked on for a bit, Molly scrunching her eyebrows and Lucas looking down at his feet. Suddenly, Lucas stopped and turned to Molly.

"Everything's changed since we went to that stupid mansion," Lucas blurted. "Danny's never around. He's been a real jerk. And I can say that 'cause he's supposed to be my best friend."

Lucas was right.

Danny had become more and more elusive since they got back from West Bubble. He didn't return phone calls. He rarely went to Quincy Park. He hardly said a word to them at school.

Molly thought part of it was that Danny was now famous, and part of it was that he had a bunch of annoying new friends like Briny Anderson. But there was something else too.

Danny had a secret, and Molly was determined to figure out what it was.

SIXTH INNING

An Unexpected Visitor

Danny was lying on the floor in the living room, frantically trying to finish his latest homework assignment from Mrs. Sherman, a three-page essay on how America's founding fathers would have hated baseball had it been invented in the late eighteenth century, when the doorbell rang.

"My God," Lydia Gurkin exclaimed when she opened the door, letting the magazine in her hand slip to the floor.

Danny looked up to see a weathered man in a Sluggers jersey and cap walk into the front hall.

It was Finchley Biggins!

"Mrs. Gurkin? Very pleased to meet you," the Sluggers' manager said, removing his baseball cap and extending his hand. His bushy mustache bobbed up and down as he spoke.

"Uh, very pleased to meet you, Mr. Biggins," Lydia said. "Come in."

Danny's mother took the manager's coat and turned to hang it up, shooting Danny a glance of total disbelief.

"We're all big fans here," Lydia said.

"Thanks, ma'am," said the manager as she ushered him into the living room. "Actually, that's what I'm here to talk about with you and your boy."

Finchley Biggins was a legend. He had been in the Sluggers organization for forty-six years, first as a player, then as a coach, and finally as the manager. Danny had caught a glimpse of him in the Sluggers' dugout when he threw out the first pitch at Winning Streak Stadium, but he had been way too nervous to actually approach him. It would have been like sauntering up to Gandhi or Einstein or George Washington.

"Can I get you some coffee or tea, Mr. Biggins?" Lydia asked. "Or how about something to eat?"

"No, thank you, ma'am," said the manager, his voice gruff but kind. He sat down on the edge of one of the living room chairs, leaning forward slightly with his hands on his knees. "That's very nice of you, though."

Danny took a seat on the couch, and his mother sat down next to him. In the past few weeks, he'd become used to the unexpected happening, but he still couldn't believe Finchley Biggins was sitting in his living room. "What could he possibly want?" Danny wondered.

Biggins clasped his hands and looked from Lydia to Danny. He had something important to say, and when Finchley Biggins had something important to say, he came right out with it.

"Son, we'd like you in the dugout for game one," said the manager. "The boys feel like you're one of us."

In the dugout!

Danny swallowed hard and looked at his mother, but the smile on her face made it clear this was not going to be a hard sell.

No Pumps

Calamity Truffaut and Mortimer Hickock rushed up to Diamond Bob as he stepped through the airport's sliding glass doors. Each man grabbed one of their boss's designer travel bags, then walked him briskly to the black car they had waiting for him.

Truffaut took the wheel and they headed into town.

Diamond Bob hated the city, with its narrow streets and tall buildings. He hated the mobs of people and the strange smells. He hated the noise and the chaos. He missed the comforting clank of his oil pumps.

"What kind of a place doesn't have oil pumps?" he muttered to himself, and as soon as he had formulated the thought, he realized the answer. "The kind of a place that produces a child like Danny Gurkin."

Diamond Bob stared out the window of the backseat of the car for a minute before he spoke.

"Boys, you were dead right," he said with a sigh. "That kid leaves it all on the field. Pure heart. Pure guts. It's downright . . . What's the word I'm looking for?"

"'Inspirational'?" offered Truffaut, glancing back at his boss in the rearview mirror.

"No. I was thinking 'sickening,'" Diamond Bob snapped. "Anyway, we have to deal with it. Is everything arranged?"

"Yes, sir, we're ready to move when you say the word," Hickock said, twisting around in his seat.

"Excellent."

They would wait until after the first two games at Winning Streak Stadium, just in case the whole distasteful operation proved unnecessary. If the Tornadoes could earn even a split, Diamond Bob had many cheaper ways to ensure victory once they got back home. There was no sense wasting resources, even if you could afford to.

The billionaire tapped his fingers against the leather

briefcase on his lap and mused over how many times he had done this before, though always in a quest to sign up top-ranked ballplayers, not hot-dog-eating kids.

Inside the briefcase was a five-page business contract drawn up by his general manager in the middle of the night—a contract that would make Danny Gurkin rich beyond his wildest dreams.

Time for Baseball

It is a well-known fact that the universe is expanding, that billions of stars are rushing away from each other at unimaginable speeds. But if you were a Sluggers fan in the final hours before the first game of the league championship series against the Texas Tornadoes, you would have had the exact opposite impression.

The Sluggers' universe had narrowed to a single point—Winning Streak Stadium—and a single moment: when rookie Sid Canova would deliver the first pitch.

The rest of the cosmos was a meaningless blur.

NOW OR NEVER! screamed the back page of the *Morning News*.

DO IT FOR MANCHESTER! implored the headline in the *Herald Times*.

¿CREE USTED EN MILAGROS? read the back page of *El Tiempo*, the Spanish-language newspaper Mr. Uribe brought into class that morning. *Do You Believe in Miracles?*

Danny did.

What else but a miracle could explain the fact that as game one began, he was sitting in the Sluggers' dugout with Finchley Biggins hunched over on his left and Boom-Boom Bigersley humming nervously on his right?

Diamond Bob's preseason boast meant the Sluggers would play four out of seven games at home, even though they hadn't had as good a record as the team from Texas.

In the dugout, just ten feet from Danny, Chico Medley was strapping on his catcher's gear like a Titan getting ready for battle. Down at the end of the dugout, Tito Calagara and P. J. Planter were popping sunflower seeds into their mouths, spitting out the shells on the steps in front of them.

Danny ran his fingers over the stitching of the official Sluggers uniform he had been given in the locker room just fifteen minutes earlier. It had the name GURKIN stenciled between the shoulders, just like for the big leaguers. The Sluggers had issued Danny the number eleven, and the team decided to make each of the ones look like a heaping hot dog standing on its head.

Danny slipped the fourth-to-last piece of Kosmic Kranberry into his mouth as Vincenzo Tagliatelle, the famous opera star, sang the national anthem; then he carefully folded up the wrapper and slipped it into his pants pocket.

"This is what it's all about." Bullet Santana's voice gushed out of the small television set in the corner of the dugout. *"The winner goes to the World Series!"*

"Never mind the World Series, Bullet," Wally Mandelberg chimed in. *"For these fans, it's all about beating the Tornadoes. This is the team that has wiped the floor with the Sluggers for the better part of a century."*

"That's too true," Santana said as the Sluggers trotted onto the field. *"And here comes Canova to the mound."*

Canova ground the ball against his uniform as Tornadoes leadoff hitter Gus Schlays circled the plate.

"Finish that second hot dog up fast, Wally," Santana told Mandelberg. *"The game's about to begin."*

Winning Streak Stadium rose to its feet as the young rookie delivered.

"A strike at the knees!" Mandelberg whispered. *"And the league championship series is under way."*

Canova had brought his best stuff. He dispatched Schlays, Tucker Riesling, and Rocco Barnworthy without breaking a sweat.

The giant screen out past center field flashed a cartoon of a knight armed with a baseball bat, charging forward on horseback.

"*El Sid! El Sid! El Sid!*" the crowd chanted.

"*A great start,*" said Mandelberg.

"*With Ruffian on the mound for the Tornadoes, this is going to be a barn burner,*" Santana said.

Unfortunately for the Sluggers, Ruffian was at his ferocious best. The crowd cheered hopefully as each Sluggers player advanced to the plate, and they groaned collectively as each was sent back to the dugout empty-handed.

Neither Canova nor Ruffian gave an inch. The first three innings passed without so much as a base hit.

As ball boy, Danny's job was to run out after a Sluggers player hit the ball and retrieve the man's bat and helmet. When someone fouled a ball back into the screen behind home plate, Danny would run out and get it.

It was incredible fun, but it wasn't rocket science, and it left Danny plenty of time to go over strategy with Biggins.

"This book shows how each of my boys does against Ruffian and all the other Tornado pitchers," Biggins explained, opening a loose-leaf folder filled with statistics.

"It tells me where they're likely to hit a curveball, what they might do with a fastball in on the hands, whether they prefer right-handed pitchers or lefties," he went on, pointing to a series of graphs and pie charts.

"Wow," said Danny. "That sure looks complicated."

"It is," the manager huffed.

In the bottom of the fourth, Boom-Boom Bigersley ripped a single to right, and P. J. Planter came to bat with a chance to do some damage.

"Whaddaya think we should do now?" Biggins asked Danny after he'd retrieved Boom-Boom's bat and helmet. The manager tilted his playbook so that Danny could see the rows of statistics. "He's got a forty-two percent chance of hitting the ball to left field. Should I tell Boom-Boom to steal second or have P.J. bunt him over?"

Danny thought for a moment. This wasn't the type of strategy he was best at.

"I think we should all turn our caps inside out and put them around backward," Danny advised the manager.

Biggins gave Danny a hard look. Then he flipped closed his book and nodded to the players on the bench.

In no time at all, every player on the team had turned his cap around and inside out. They were quite a sight, and more than a little off-putting for the all-business Tornadoes.

"You know, on paper you've got to give the Texans the edge in pitching, hitting, fielding, strategy, and experience," Mandelberg said. *"But the Sluggers definitely have them beat on good vibes."*

"Yeah, and of course we've got Danny Gurkin," said Santana. *"I'd say all in all, it's about even."*

But the hat stunt wasn't enough to faze Ruffian. He fooled Planter on a mean split-fingered fastball, getting him to bounce into a feeble double play to end the inning.

"Sorry," Danny said to Biggins.

"Don't sweat it," the manager shrugged. "Half of my ideas don't work either."

The frustration in the Sluggers' dugout grew with every pitch from Ruffian. Fastballs, change-ups, and curveballs shot past the helpless batters and thudded into Mungo McBust's waiting mitt.

A sigh went up from the bench as Sam Slasky struck out with two men on in the fifth, ending the team's best chance of the night. Slasky stalked back to the dugout and kicked the watercooler.

On the other side of the field, Canova's sparkling performance was starting to get to the Tornadoes as well. They questioned every call from the umpire. They stalled at the plate, stepping out of the batter's box just as the rookie went into his windup.

In the top of the seventh, Gus Schlays broke his bat over his knee after striking out for the third straight time. He hurled the broken handle toward the mound, catching Canova in the cheek.

In an instant, the Sluggers rookie had Schlays by the

shirt, and both teams were piling out onto the dugout steps. Medley pulled Schlays and Canova apart as Biggins and Tornadoes manager C. J. Le Swine rushed out to calm their angry players.

Fists clenched, the teams growled and turned back to their seats.

"The frustration is starting to boil over down there," Santana said.

"We're still scoreless after six and a half innings," Mandelberg said. *"It's hard to see how either team is going to break through."*

Danny stuck the Kosmic Kranberry to the roof of his mouth as Tito Calagara came to the plate in the Sluggers' half of the seventh. He split it in two and stuck the pieces on the end of his tongue.

"Base hit!" Mandelberg shouted.

Ruffian flared his nostrils and screamed in Swedish as Bruce Minsky stepped to the plate. The veins on the pitcher's forehead were bulging and his eyes were red.

"Yikes! That can't be good for your health," Santana said.

Minsky ground his feet into the dirt, then stared out at the crazed pitcher.

"Strike one!" yelled the umpire after a ninety-six-mile-per-hour fastball.

The next pitch was the same as the first, only a little bit faster.

"Strike two!"

Minsky stepped out of the batter's box and took a deep breath.

"Hit it, Bruceeeeee!" a little girl yelled from just behind the dugout.

"You're the man, Minsky!" her grandfather screamed from the seat next to her.

Minsky stepped back in and glared at Ruffian. He pounded his bat against the plate.

Whoosh!

The ball shot off Minsky's bat and up into the air. It soared out past the left fielder and toward the outfield wall. Fifty-five thousand heads swung toward the outfield as Minsky stumbled to first.

"That ball is way, way back," Mandelberg said. *"It's going, going . . ."*

"Gone!" Santana yelled as the ball disappeared into the stands. *"A home run for Minsky. The Sluggers lead two—nothing! How about that!"*

A joyous cry went up from the stands, and the stadium shook as people in the crowd leapt into each other's arms. Ruffian slammed his glove against his hip as McBust ran out to talk to him.

As the Sluggers took the field for the top of the eighth, the atmosphere at the stadium was electric. The team was closing in on its first-ever play-off victory against the Tornadoes, and there was no room for error. Danny knew exactly what to do.

He told the Sluggers bench to stretch their arms out in front of them and waggle their hands like zombies. Then he had the entire team cross their legs left over right, then right over left.

For C. J. Le Swine, it was the last straw.

The Texas manager marched out to home plate to complain to the umpire about the Sluggers' antics.

"It's not right," Le Swine insisted, his enormous beer belly jutting out toward the umpire. "Them boys are trying to put a hex on us. We don't appreciate it one bit!"

Biggins shot out of the Sluggers' dugout to argue his side.

"I've been in this game for most of my life, and I tell

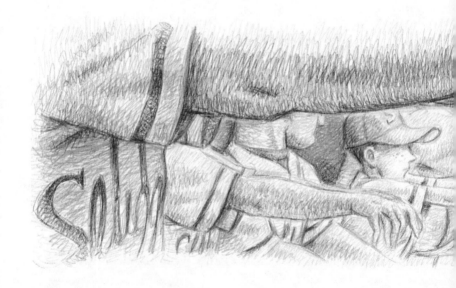

you there is nothing in the rule book that says what we're doing is illegal," he said calmly.

The umpires huddled together, but Biggins was right.

In the entire 208-page *Official Rules of Baseball*, there was not a single mention at all of zombie hexing, synchronized leg-crossing, or putting your caps on backward in the dugout being illegal.

Le Swine trudged off the field mumbling to himself.

In the stands, fifty-five thousand rowdy fans greeted him by waggling their arms like zombies.

The Sluggers couldn't come up with any offense in the bottom of the eighth, and the score remained 2–0 as the final inning opened.

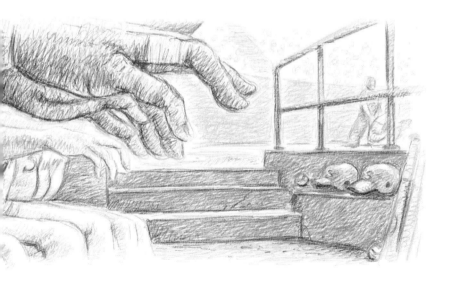

On the mound in place of Canova was Baxter Orejuela, the Sluggers' best relief pitcher.

"The Tornadoes are down to their final chance," Mandelberg said. *"It doesn't get any better than this. This is why we pay our taxes, go to work, drink lots of milk, and look both ways before we cross the street. It's for moments like this."*

The crowd was on its feet. Danny paced in front of the bench. Biggins got up and abruptly sat back down.

Leopold Doberman, the Tornadoes' ninth-place hitter, was up first.

"Popped him up!" Mandelberg exclaimed. *"One away."*

Gus Schlays was up next. A rumble went up in the stands as the fans stomped their feet.

Schlays's bat barely moved as Orejuela threw three bullets right down the middle of the plate.

"Struck him out!" screamed Santana, struggling to be heard over the din. *"Two away!"*

"If only Orejuela can hold on . . . ," Mandelberg said as Tucker Riesling stepped to the plate.

Smack!

The ball sprang off Riesling's bat, zipped through Orejuela's legs, and bounced into center field for a single.

The crowd gasped.

"Oh, boy, that was a shot," Santana moaned.

"*Two outs, one on. Baxter's got to be careful here,*" Mandelberg said. "*The tying run is coming to the plate, and just look who it is.*"

Rocco Barnworthy stood in the on-deck circle, swinging his bat ferociously. He had been hitless in three at bats against Canova, and he was looking to make amends.

He kicked the dirt in the batter's box slowly, ignoring the cascade of boos from the stands around him.

"*I hope Rocco bought some earplugs with all that money Diamond Bob is paying him,*" Santana said sourly.

Barnworthy fouled off the first two pitches, then watched as Orejuela threw the next three in the dirt. The count was full at three balls and two strikes.

Danny held his breath as Orejuela released the ball.

"*And down the line it goes!*" Mandelberg groaned. "*Color me purple! That's going to be a double. Oh, doctor, how about that? Men on second and third. This is way too close for comfort.*"

The crowd fell silent as a lusty cheer erupted in the Tornadoes' dugout. Orejuela bit his lip and stared straight ahead.

"*It's all on the line here, Wally,*" Santana said. "*Top of the ninth, a century of hope on Orejuela's shoulders, and Mungo McBust coming to the plate.*"

McBust strode out toward the batter's box, but he didn't stop there. The Tornadoes' catcher stalked halfway out to the mound, pointing his bat at Orejuela ominously until the umpire came out to stop him.

Danny couldn't watch. He closed his eyes and wrapped his arms around his body, then pushed the Kosmic Kranberry into the gap between his two front teeth.

"Don't give him anything to hit! Don't give him anything to hit," Danny murmured to himself.

But Orejuela didn't hear him.

The pitch was straight down the middle, and McBust crushed it. It shot over the outstretched glove of Boom-Boom Bigersley and out into right field as Riesling raced around to score.

Winning Streak Stadium held its breath as Rocco Barnworthy rounded third and headed for home. Out in right field, Thelonius Star gobbled up the ball and came up ready to fire.

"Barnworthy is flying in with the tying run!" Mandelberg screamed. *"Here's the throw from Star!"*

The ball shot out of the little right fielder's hand on a beeline toward home plate. It bounced once on the soft infield grass and plunked into Chico Medley's mitt, just as Barnworthy slammed into him with the force of a freight train.

The two men collapsed in a cloud of dust.

"Safe or out? Safe or out?" Santana whispered urgently.

The hulking umpire crouched intently over the two men as the dust cleared.

Barnworthy lay on his front, craning his head toward the umpire. Medley lay on his back, his mask in the dirt beside him. His face was streaked with sweat and grit.

Slowly, Medley lifted his giant arm in the air.

A hush fell over the stadium, and the players froze on the dugout steps as Medley opened his mitt. Clutched firmly inside was a gleaming white baseball.

"Y'ER OUT!" screamed the umpire, punching his fist in the air as the stadium shook with joy.

"*I can't believe what I just saw!*" Mandelberg's voice boomed out of the dugout television. "*Two to one! Two to one! Hell has frozen over. My dog is a cat, and the Sluggers have taken the first game from the Tornadoes! The Sluggers win!*"

Danny hadn't heard a word of it.

He and the rest of the team had already poured onto the field to celebrate.

The Lost Years of Lou Smegny

Somewhere in the frigid tundra of northern Canada, not far from the Arctic Circle, lives a tiny tribe of fishermen whose people have never once heard of the Sluggers and couldn't tell you the difference between a run batted in and a reindeer.

What they could tell you about, assuming, of course, you were fluent in Nabutee, their native tongue, is the famous day 1,296 full moons ago when a painfully stooped young man with wild eyes and a cardboard box full of chewing gum showed up outside their ancestors' igloos.

The Nabutee people called the man Seeyamoora, which means "One Who Turns Up Unexpectedly." He had clearly been through some terrible ordeal, and he was taken in by the tribal chief without question, in keeping with the local custom of hospitality.

The man was given the finest health care nineteenth-century Nabutees knew how to render. Basically, a warm blanket, a raging fire, and an extra-large helping of breaded fish sticks, the greatest delicacy in the Nabutees' rather limited culinary repertoire.

The fish sticks didn't improve the man's posture at all, and they did nothing to stop his eyes from jiggling about in their sockets like beach balls bouncing on the nose of a seal. But the Nabutees' generosity was enough to keep him content, and he remained with the tribe for the next thirty-six years.

In that time, Seeyamoora built a home and learned to speak the Nabutee language, but he never revealed the terrible secret that had brought him so far from his own people.

In fact, he didn't mingle much at all, and for their part, the Nabutees were content to let the young man keep to himself.

Sure, they were intrigued by the fact that Seeyamoora had hardly aged a day in all the time he had been there, but foreigners were a strange lot, and it was extremely impolite in Nabutee culture to pry. In any event, the Nabutees had enjoyed a string of remarkably prosperous fishing seasons since Seeyamoora arrived, and as their chief quite wisely pointed out, there was no reason to rock the canoe.

Poached Eggs and Disbelief

If game one had been a disappointment to Diamond Bob, game two was a disaster. Time after time, Vince Spagu's knuckleball fluttered into Chico Medley's mitt like a bat flying home in the night.

He threw 153 pitches in all, and when the last of them floated past Mungo McBust, the Sluggers had a 6–2 victory and a 2–0 series lead. They were halfway home!

All over town, the same unthinkable thought began

to form in the minds of Sluggers fans, a whisper in the brain, a low murmur just south of consciousness.

This could be our year!

Thoughts were flooding through the minds of the Tornadoes players as well. They were a confident team, but some were starting to wonder.

How could the Sluggers play so well? How could the invincible Tornadoes lose to a team of fallen monks and nineteen-year-old rookies? How could a former supermarket clerk throw such an elusive knuckleball?

Diamond Bob knew the answer, of course, and he was darn sure he was going to do something about it.

"It's Danny Gurkin!" he sighed from the presidential suite of the Château Regency the next morning as he, Truffaut, and Hickock munched on a breakfast of poached eggs, warm croissants, apricot marmalade, and fresh-squeezed orange juice.

The food was remarkably expensive, but it caught in the throat. All in all, the three men would have much preferred burritos. They resolved to order in from the House of Tacos from that moment on.

Even down two games to none, the mood at the Château Regency was not desperate. The oil tycoon had many ways to fight back, not all of them entirely legal. After all, you don't get to be an oil tycoon without bending a few rules along the way.

The contract for Danny Gurkin's loyalty lay on the

table between the three men, and Diamond Bob looked over the numbers one last time.

How much was too much for the most valuable fan in history?

The businessman grimaced as he held the contract up to the light. Then he took out a pen and added another zero to the end of the figure his general manager had come up with.

"That ought to do it," Diamond Bob said with a sigh. The amount was so staggeringly big that Truffaut and Hickock nearly spat out their food.

"There's . . . no way . . . he can turn that down," Hickock stuttered, struggling to force the last bit of croissant down his throat.

"We shall see," said the oil tycoon. "We shall see."

A Special Invitation

The letter inviting Danny and his parents to be honored at the ballroom of the Château Regency came on the afternoon after the Sluggers' game two victory. It did not have any postage on it, and there was no number to call to RSVP.

"Hmmm," said Lydia Gurkin. "This must have been slipped under the door."

The letter made clear that the award, sponsored by

the Diamante Group Ltd., was for the entire Gurkin family, even Max. The ceremony would begin in less than three hours.

Lydia called Harold at work and both agreed it would be a good idea to attend, even though neither of them had any idea what the Diamante Group Ltd. might be. It certainly looked important, judging by the invitation.

"It's pretty quiet here today anyway," Harold Gurkin said from Frompovich headquarters. The campaign had ground to a halt during the play-offs. It was simply a waste of time to try to get the mayor's message on jobs and health care out to a city that was completely consumed by baseball.

When Danny, Max, and their parents got to the lobby of the opulent hotel that evening, the manager directed the Gurkins down a marble hallway.

"Right through there," he said formally, gesturing toward two large wooden doors. "The Marie Antoinette Ballroom."

Harold Gurkin pulled the doors open and was surprised to find the enormous room nearly completely dark. There were dozens of round tables, each laid with fancy silverware, and there was a dais set up at the front, but there didn't seem to be anybody on it. The Gurkins stood in the entrance of the great room and peered around.

"Maybe we're early." Harold shrugged as Danny, Lydia, and Max gawked up at the large crystal chandeliers.

"Not at all," said a deep Southern voice from out of the gloom. "You are exactly on time."

The Offer

Harold led his family through the ballroom, pushing aside the dinner chairs as they navigated their way around the tables. As they got closer to the front of the room, Danny could make out the silhouette of a tall cowboy hat. The man under it was sitting on a chair between two other men, and he had what looked like a briefcase in front of him.

"Mr. and Mrs. Gurkin, I presume," said the man in the ten-gallon hat, rising to greet them. He extended a meaty hand adorned with the largest diamond ring Danny had ever seen.

"And you must be Max," the man added in what he hoped would sound like a grandfatherly tone. "We do our homework, you know!"

The entire Gurkin family stood and smiled at the wealthy-looking gentleman.

Everyone, that is, except Danny.

His eyes were trained on the two other men at the table, one large and sweaty, the other small and weaselly, with a dark goatee. Where had he seen them before?

"Let me introduce myself," the wealthy man continued, taking off his hat and holding it against his chest. He made sure that the sparkle of his diamond ring found its way into Harold's and Lydia's eyes.

"My name is Bob," the man said at last. "Bob Honeysuckle the Fourth to be precise. I brought you here to talk about your very clever son."

Harold, Lydia, and Max Gurkin's jaws dropped at once.

"Not *the* Bob Honeysuckle the Fourth?" Danny's father said slowly. "Not . . . Diamond Bob?"

Here was the living incarnation of everything that was wrong with baseball, everything that was wrong with the planet, everything that was wrong with humankind! Here was the man who—along with his forefathers—had snuffed out the hopes and dreams of Zechariah and Ebenezer Gurkin and countless other Sluggers fans through the ages.

"The one and only!" Diamond Bob grinned. It was almost amusing to see the shock on the faces of the Gurkin clan. Power really was a fun thing to play around with, Diamond Bob thought.

The two other men at the table sat beside their boss with painted-on smiles. The smaller one was wiping something off his mouth, and the larger man had what appeared to be a fast-food wrapper clenched in his fist.

Danny narrowed his eyes and took a closer look at the wrapper. It was crumpled up in a ball, but the writing was unmistakable:

HOUSE OF TACOS read the yellow and brown lettering.

Danny's mind was whirring. The diamond-studded hood ornament on the black car. The strange license plate, DB-IV. The burrito wrappers.

It was all starting to make sense.

"Hey, you're the two guys who have been following me for the past three weeks!" he blurted. "The guys who eat all the tacos!"

Harold and Lydia looked alarmed, but Diamond Bob chuckled dismissively.

"Oh, we don't like to use that word," he laughed, waving his hands in the air in front of him. "Let me introduce Mortimer Hickock and Calamity Truffaut. My employees haven't been following you, Daniel. They've been scouting you. They've been trying to find out what you're made of so we know whether you are the type of young man we'd want . . . in our organization."

"In your organization?" Lydia Gurkin said. "I don't understand."

Diamond Bob turned to Danny and smiled.

"You see, Danny, the Tornadoes are in the market

for a lucky fan, and . . . well, we like your stuff. We think it's time you brought your talents to a professional outfit."

Danny couldn't believe what he was hearing. Root for the Tornadoes? Forsake the Sluggers?

Danny turned to his parents.

It was preposterous. It was ridiculous. It was . . . a lot of money.

Harold and Lydia Gurkin were both staring at a piece of paper that Calamity Truffaut had taken out of his boss's briefcase and placed on the table in front of them. In particular, their eyes were drawn to a dollar figure in the center of the page.

The number was as long as a centipede and many times more beautiful.

"I think you'll agree it's a most generous offer," Diamond Bob said, leaning back smugly in his chair.

Moment of Truth

"Are you nuts?" Danny growled between clenched teeth, only faintly aware of the loud gulping noises his father was making next to him, like the sound a fish makes when it's plucked out of the water.

"Now, son," Mortimer Hickock interjected. "You should weigh your decision carefully. Don't rush to judgment. A boy has to think of his future at a time like this, isn't that right, Mr. Gurkin?"

"Mnnh," said Harold. He was still staring at the contract, grabbing his shirt collar in an effort to let more oxygen into his lungs. Lydia's brows were furrowed.

"I'll root for the Tornadoes for that kind of money," shouted Max. "Take me!"

"Shut up, bonehead!" Danny yelled.

"That's very kind of you, kid, but we want your brother," said Diamond Bob. "I'll give you five dollars if you wear a Tornadoes cap. How about that?"

Max looked crestfallen.

"Let me get this straight, Mr. Honeysuckle," Harold said. "You'd be willing to give my son all that money just to be a Tornadoes fan? All he would have to do is root for them?"

"It's unusual, I know," Diamond Bob said. "But it all makes sense if you think about it. We see Danny as a sort of free agent, just like Rocco Barnworthy or any other great talent. In fact, your son will be the first free-agent *fan* in big-league history, and it's about time, don't you think?"

Harold Gurkin stared at Diamond Bob but didn't say anything.

"But I don't want to root for the Tornadoes," Danny protested.

"Want, want, want." Diamond Bob chuckled.

"What is *want*? Do you *want* a fancy new bike? Do you *want* every video game known to man? Do you *want* a private plane? These are not matters for an eleven-year-old to consider on his own. That's why I've invited the entire family to this little meeting."

"But our family has rooted for the Sluggers forever," Danny said.

"Not forever," Diamond Bob corrected. "Just a long time. My family used to sell saddles door-to-door, but now we're exceedingly wealthy oilmen. You see? People change."

Diamond Bob twisted his enormous diamond ring around his finger, shooting a cold beam of light into Harold Gurkin's eye.

"He has a point," Danny's father said.

The idea of rooting for the enemy made Danny sick to his stomach, but he had to admit it was an awfully large amount of money. Max certainly didn't seem to have a problem with it, and even his father appeared to be bending to the idea.

"Even if I wanted to do it," Danny said, "it's impossible. I hate the Tornadoes. I'm a Sluggers fan. How can I root for a team I hate?"

Diamond Bob leaned back in his chair and let out a hearty laugh.

"Oh, children really are precious," he said, glancing from Harold to Lydia, who were both smiling nervously.

"Danny, do you think I expect all of my employees to love me, or to love the Tornadoes? Of course not. That's why God invented a little thing we call money."

"He sure did," said Harold. His voice was soft, and his eyes were still fixed on the contract.

"Why don't we give you and your parents a few minutes to talk it over in private. We'll be right over there," Diamond Bob said confidently, rising to his feet.

"We don't have to talk it over," Danny said, but he felt a tug on his shoulder.

"Danny!" his father said sharply. "Why don't we sit down."

Diamond Bob and his assistants walked to the corner of the ballroom and huddled together as the Gurkins took places at the table.

Danny looked from one member of the family to the other.

"Danny, I'm as big a Sluggers fan as the next man," Harold Gurkin whispered. "But that is a heck of a lot of money. It would pay for your college education, and we could buy a big apartment, a nicer car, take a very long vacation."

"Yeah, and I could drop out of school and start my own rock band," Max said breathlessly.

Danny turned to his mother.

"It's up to you, Danny" she said. "Whatever you decide, we're with you."

227

Danny glanced down at the contract on the table. It was a lot of money!

He thought of the fading black-and-white photo he kept in his room of a young Zechariah Gurkin crying in his seat behind home plate after the Sluggers missed the play-offs in 1907. The umpire had called their last player out on strikes before the opposing pitcher even delivered the pitch.

Then Danny remembered the photo of his grandpa Ebenezer giving a thumbs-up sign from his hospital bed after a brush with frostbite from sitting too long in the snow-covered bleachers in 1934, waiting for the season to resume.

He thought about poor Manchester Boddlebrooks keeling over in the locker room after the Sluggers' only championship, and of his evil brother, Skidmore, and all the damage his greed had caused.

"Just look what happened to him!" Danny thought. After he lost his empire, Skidmore was forced to go to work on the assembly line of the Ball-Park Mustard Goo Conglomerate he had once owned. He retired a broken man, moving to the only elderly community in Florida where gum-chewing was strictly forbidden.

Danny looked up to see Diamond Bob sauntering back to the table. The oil tycoon snapped his cell phone shut and smiled while Hickock and Truffaut stood motionless at their boss's shoulders.

"Danny, you tell Mr. Honeysuckle whether you'd like to accept his offer," Lydia Gurkin said.

Danny turned to the oil tycoon and said the most honest thing he could think of.

"I'd rather eat my shoes."

SEVENTH INNING

Friendship Follies

Molly and Lucas were just turning the corner onto Wyatt Avenue on their way to school the next morning when Danny caught up to them. He couldn't wait to tell them about Diamond Bob!

"Hey! I haven't seen you guys forever," Danny said quickly, catching his breath. "You're not going to believe what happened to me last night."

The two friends turned around slowly.

"I can hardly wait," Molly said flatly; then she turned to Lucas.

"Maybe he got picked to star in a Hollywood movie," she said.

"Or maybe he saw a flying saucer," Lucas offered.

"Maybe he was elected president of the United States," Molly suggested, putting her finger on her chin thoughtfully. "No, I think I would have heard about that already."

"Ha, ha, ha," Danny said. "No. Seriously, you'll never guess. I met Diamond Bob Honeysuckle the Fourth. *The* Diamond Bob Honeysuckle the Fourth! And I told him I'd rather eat my shoes!"

Molly and Lucas stood and listened as Danny told them the whole story.

"That's great, Danny," Lucas said. "That's really cool."

"Yeah, that's really cool," Molly said.

There was a long pause. Molly pulled on the strap of her backpack and Lucas looked down at his feet.

"Hey, Danny, I've got to run," Lucas said, turning around abruptly.

Danny turned to Molly.

"What's eating him?" he asked.

"Well, Danny, it's not exactly like you've been around much lately," Molly said.

"What do you mean?" Danny replied. "I've been busy, you know."

"Yeah, I know," Molly said. "So busy you never call, you never meet us after school, you never invite us to parties at stupid Briny Anderson's house."

Danny looked down at the ground. He knew she was right, sort of, but he didn't want to admit it, not even to Molly.

He *was* busy! It's wasn't easy being the good-luck charm for an entire city!

When he looked up, Molly was staring at him sharply.

"So busy that you've never even told us what happened at the Boddlebrooks mansion?" she added.

"What are you talking about?" Danny replied defensively.

"I saw your face when you came out of that study," Molly said. "You were white as a sheet. It isn't like you not to mention it once in all this time, Danny. How did you get away from Mr. Sycamore? What did you see in there? What did you find in there?"

Danny gulped.

"Nothing," he said meekly.

"Don't tell me, then," Molly huffed.

She turned to walk away but suddenly whirled around to face Danny again.

"Just remember, Danny—I'm the one who showed you the article about the Boddlebrooks mansion. It's my father who made you famous," she said, pointing at her chest. "I wish I'd never told you about that stupid house in the first place!"

Home-Field Advantage

Like any good businessman, Diamond Bob had a backup plan, and the minute his jet hit the ground back in Texas, he set the scheme in motion.

"If we can't steal the Sluggers' lucky kid, we're just going to have to take luck out of the equation," he explained to his board of directors at an emergency meeting that very morning, slamming his fist down on the table.

"That little pest won't be here for the next three games," Diamond Bob continued. He had made sure of that by banning the Sluggers from bringing their own ball boy into his stadium. Just to be extra cautious, he'd bought up all the empty seats and posted photos of Danny at the entrance with instructions to turn him away if for any reason he did show up.

"I'd like to see them deal with what I've got planned for them without him!" Diamond Bob snorted. Then he whipped out a notepad and began ticking off the list of measures he wanted implemented immediately.

"I want a strong set of eyes out in center field, I want the balls taken care of, and we'll need to order up a few cases of petroleum jelly," said the oil magnate, looking up to make sure his executives were taking good notes.

"I want the bench in the visitors' dugout lowered to a foot off the ground, and I want all the water in the Sluggers' locker room trucked in especially for the occasion," Diamond Bob went on, pausing for emphasis.

"Preferably from a river near one of my oil plants," he added. "We need the dirtiest water we can find."

The plan worked to perfection.

With a spy perched out in the scoreboard behind center field to steal Chico Medley's signs in game three, the Tornadoes' batters knew exactly what was coming, and they crushed nearly everything thrown at them by poor Barr Randall, the Sluggers' starting pitcher.

"This is like watching a Wiffle-ball game," Wally Mandelberg commented.

"Yeah," said Santana. *"And Randall's the ball!"*

Every pitch thrown by Tornado pitcher Stagwitt Jones was spiked with a dollop of Vaseline, just enough to make the ball dart through the strike zone at unpredictable angles, without being spotted by the umpires. He was completely unhittable, and the Sluggers lost 11–0.

By game four, nearly every Slugger had come down with stomach cramps from drinking the runoff water from Diamond Bob's Tierra Quemada refinery, and their knees ached from sitting on the ridiculously uncomfortable bench he'd installed.

They came to the plate barely able to lift their arms, and one by one they trudged away in dismay.

In the top of the eighth, with the Sluggers already losing 6–1, Boom-Boom Bigersley struck out so feebly that even he gasped in disbelief.

"That's the worst effort I've seen out of Boom-Boom since he broke his vow of silence," said Mandelberg.

On the way back to the dugout, Bigersley doubled over in pain. He felt as if a locomotive had run through his stomach.

"The Sluggers must not like this Texas air," Santana offered. *"They don't look like themselves at all."*

"Maybe it's just a matter of things evening out," said Mandelberg. *"I mean, this is one heck of a good Tornadoes club. Maybe the Sluggers are just getting outclassed. It certainly wouldn't be the first time, Bullet."*

"Wally, I really hope you're wrong about that," Santana replied. *"And I hope that somewhere out there, Danny Gurkin is watching. Get that boy some hot dogs, pronto!"*

Of course Danny was watching, and what was worse, he had wasted his second-to-last piece of Kosmic Kranberry during the game three loss. There was just one piece left, and Danny decided to save that for the Sluggers' return to Winning Streak Stadium. The boys would have to win game five on their own, or there wouldn't be enough gum to get the team over the hump.

In his luxury box, Diamond Bob was beside himself with joy. He slapped his ten-gallon hat against his hip and hollered into the night sky.

As the fans at Tornado Stadium cheered below him, the oil man flipped a latch on his enormous diamond ring. Inside was a faded black-and-white photograph of his beloved great-granddaddy, the original Diamond Bob Honeysuckle.

How proud he would be!

"Old man, you ain't seen nothing yet," Diamond Bob mumbled under his breath.

The Gurkin Sours

It was hard to figure out exactly when things started to fall apart. Was it the fight with Molly and Lucas? The thrashing the Sluggers took in games three and four? The way Danny lied when Molly asked him point-blank what he saw in the Boddlebrooks study?

Whatever it was, Danny felt as low as a snake, both about the Sluggers and himself.

What was worse, his confidence was completely shot.

Why had he wasted his second-to-last stick of Kosmic Kranberry on game three? How would he get the

Sluggers two more wins with just one stick of gum left? Why had he taken his two best friends for granted for all these weeks? Why did he have to be such a big jerk?

The newspaper headlines on the morning after the game four collapse didn't help Danny's mood any.

BOY WONDER? the *Herald Times* read.

HOT DOG, HOT AIR! the *Morning News* blared.

THE GURKIN SOURS! screamed the back page of the *Daily Bugler*. Danny hated pickle jokes, but this was really the lowest.

On WBUB's *Morning SportsBeat,* callers speculated about why Danny and the Sluggers were failing so miserably.

"The boy's lost his touch," said a banker named Fred.

"He's become caught up in the fame," said a grandfather on Jackson Avenue.

One caller even claimed to have spotted Danny stepping on at least three cracks in the sidewalk. *An outright lie!*

"Good going, wonder boy!" said Max when Danny got home from school. "Sarah McAllister just dumped me."

An hour before game five, Danny walked down to Willie's cart alone, his Sluggers cap pulled down low over his eyes. The line was long, but not nearly as long as it had been when the Sluggers were winning every game. The luster was off the sauerkraut, so to speak.

"Hey, man," Willie said when Danny approached. "Gotta win tonight, right?"

"Yep," Danny replied. "It's a must-win. A must-win."

"You feel good or what?" Willie asked as an assistant prepared Danny's hot dogs.

"I guess," Danny lied. "They can do it."

"So, you gonna catch the game with Molly and Lucas?" Willie asked, grabbing the hot dogs from his assistant and handing them over to Danny. "Come to think of it, where are Molly and Lucas? I never see you guys together anymore."

"I've been sort of busy." Danny sighed. "And, uh, well, they're sort of angry with me."

Danny told Willie about the showdown outside school and how Molly and Lucas didn't even care when he told them about the meeting with Diamond Bob. He didn't mention Molly's grilling about the study.

Willie shook his head as he listened to the story.

"My friend," he said finally, "if I've learned one thing in life, it's that you've got to be humble. No matter how famous you become, you've always got to remember your friends."

Willie was right. Even though he had just been named Vendor of the Century by *Hot Dog Weekly*, he still walked to his stand every morning and gave extra onion goop to all his old customers.

"If they ever talk to me again, I'll keep that in mind," Danny said glumly.

"They'll get over it." Willie chuckled. "It's like my brother always says: 'Stuff happens.'"

"Isn't your brother in jail?" Danny asked.

"Yeah." Willie shrugged. "So he knows what he's talking about."

Diamond Bob's Masterpiece

There have been some great strokes of deception in human history, but none more breathtaking than the one Diamond Bob Honeysuckle IV orchestrated in game five. Games three and four — with their stolen signs, muddy drinking water, and uncomfortable seating arrangements — were mere parlor tricks in comparison to the masterpiece of trickery that was this crucial fifth act.

If cheating had its own museum, game five would have had a wing all to itself.

Danny and his family were pressed close to the living room television, hoping against hope that the Sluggers could find a way to win. Even Harold had taken the night off from the campaign to be home for the all-important game. Danny had found a twice-chewed wad of Kosmic Kranberry stuck under his bedside table and was trying to get by with that so he'd have the full stick left for game six.

Lydia Gurkin had washed and rewashed the dishes every other inning. Harold had his fingers crossed, and even Max had stuck a pencil under his nose.

It seemed to be helping.

The color had returned to the Sluggers players' cheeks since they started drinking bottled water instead of the silty stuff Diamond Bob had provided for the locker room. Finchley Biggins had purchased several dozen phone books for his boys to sit on to make the dugout bench more comfortable, and Chico Medley had taught his pitchers a complicated new series of hand signals to make it harder for the Tornadoes to steal his signs.

The Sluggers looked like a new team.

By the eighth, the score was tied at four runs apiece, and even the nonchalant Tornadoes fans were biting their nails and sitting on the edge of their seats. The Gurkins were perched in a semicircle around the television, frozen with excitement.

Bigersley led off the inning with a shot into the gap, pumping his fist from first to encourage Spanky Mazoo to do the same. Mazoo looked bored as he let the first two pitches whiz by him for strikes, but he didn't make the same mistake a third time.

"There's a shot down the line!" Wally Mandelberg gushed, pounding his hand against his announcer's desk. *"Bigersley on third, Mazoo on first, and just one down. This is not a good time to run to the bathroom, huh, Bullet?"*

"You got that right, Wally," Santana replied. *"I've been holding it in since the fourth, but I'm not going anywhere. The only problem is, I'm so nervous I can barely watch."*

Suddenly, the Gurkins' television set blinked off!

A second later, all the lights in the house flickered and went out!

"No!" Danny and Max screamed in unison.

"What in blazes?" Harold snapped, jumping up. "It must be a fuse."

Lydia looked out the window and gasped.

"It's a blackout!" she said.

Sure enough, the entire city was dark. Not a bulb burning. Not a television glowing in the distance.

"Oh my God," Danny screamed. "What do we do?"

"Quick, quick, get a radio," Harold said. "One that takes batteries."

Danny had a small hand radio in his room that he'd gotten with his subscription to *Sporting Digest.* He raced through the darkness to find it.

By the time he got back to the living room, his parents had lit a few candles, and the family gathered around the small table as Danny tried to find the Sluggers game.

He turned the dial to where WBUB was supposed to be, but instead of the familiar sounds of baseball, the station was blaring country music.

"What the . . . ?" Harold said furiously.

In his perch at Tornado Stadium, Diamond Bob leaned back and laughed as he hadn't laughed in years. It had all gone so perfectly he could pinch himself.

It had only taken a single phone call to Ultimate Power, Inc., the electric company subsidiary of the Diamante Group Ltd., for Diamond Bob to cut electricity to a quarter of the country. Danny Gurkin's quarter of the country, to be precise.

The power-company executives would have to come up with an excuse for the blackout later on.

"These things happen, after all," Diamond Bob chuckled to himself.

He was feeling like a million bucks. Make that a billion bucks, actually!

Secretly buying a controlling stake in WBUB radio the day before was the stroke of genius that made the scheme so beautiful. Diamond Bob's first act as principal shareholder was to schedule a three-hour country music tribute!

The important thing was to make sure Danny Gurkin had no way of watching or listening to the Sluggers game. You can't be lucky if you don't know what's going on, Diamond Bob figured, and he was dead right.

The Tornadoes scored three times in the bottom of the eighth inning, then shut the Sluggers down in the ninth for a 7–4 victory and a three-games-to-two series lead. They had turned the tables on the Sluggers entirely.

They were just one win away from the World Series!

The power came back on in Danny's apartment and

every other apartment in town just in time to see the Tornadoes players run onto the field to celebrate.

Danny, Max, Harold, and Lydia sat in silent disbelief.

"*Our goose is cooked,*" Mandelberg groaned.

"*Another year of heartache staring us right in the face,*" Santana agreed, weeping.

Danny's Big Choice

Everyone in town took the game five loss hard. You could see it in the long faces on the streets. You could hear it in the sad shuffling of feet.

It was there in the deep sigh of an old man searching his pockets for change, in the glance to the sky of a mother waiting for the light to turn green.

One hundred and eight years! When would it finally be the Sluggers turn?

Nobody took the loss harder than Danny, of course.

It was all his fault!

Danny walked out of John J. Barnibus and made his way slowly to Quincy Park, the last stick of Kosmic Kranberry clutched in his hand. He walked with his head down, barely noticing the cars zipping past or the chill in the October air.

Misery is all-consuming stuff.

Danny rubbed his finger over the bubble-gum wrapper. It was hard to believe that three full packs of magic gum had dwindled to this. Why hadn't he used one less piece during the regular season? Why hadn't he paid more attention to division in math class?

"Stupid! Stupid! Stupid!" Danny berated himself.

In a little over twenty-four hours, he would be sitting in the Sluggers' dugout for game six, surrounded by a team whose heart had been ripped out in the most disastrous road trip since Custer's last stand.

Danny didn't even know if they would want him around anymore.

"Some lucky kid I am," he mumbled. "What a joke!"

He hadn't felt this small since he'd seen that astronomy movie at the science museum.

"In relation to the universe, each of us is tinier than a grain of sand on the most distant beach of the most unimaginably large ocean," the narrator had said. "We're tinier than the smallest amoeba swimming aimlessly along in that ocean. I'm talking small."

Feeling like an amoeba would have been a step in the right direction, Danny thought. At least they were surrounded by lots of other amoebas.

Danny was all alone.

There were no more interview requests, no more party invitations, no more piles of fan mail. Briny

Anderson hadn't phoned Danny once since the Sluggers began their slide.

Danny turned into Quincy Park and made his way toward a large oak tree behind the basketball courts. It was his favorite spot in the park, but that wasn't why he was headed there today.

He needed help, and there were only two people in the world he could truly count on. If they showed up, that is.

Danny, Molly, and Lucas hadn't said a word to each other since the fight outside school. Not a "Hello" after the losses in games three and four, not a "How're you doing?" after the blackout in game five. Even in Mrs. Sherman's history class, Molly and Lucas kept to themselves.

Danny was sure they both hated him, and he didn't blame them.

Still, a sacred pact is a sacred pact and a secret password is a secret password.

"They have to come," Danny said to himself, and for the first time he realized how nervous he was. This could be the most important meeting of his life, Danny thought. More important than the one with Diamond Bob. More significant than meeting Mayor Frompovich. There was still time to back out, but Danny knew that wasn't an option. He had made up his mind and there was no going back.

Danny threw his backpack down on the grass, sat down under the oak tree, and waited.

Not since Molly's parents had split up three years earlier had someone invoked the secret password of the Order of the Watermelon, the club Danny, Molly, and Lucas had set up when they'd first become friends. There were just three members.

Right before he left school, Danny had taped two identical notes on Molly's and Lucas's lockers. The notes said simply "4 o'clock. V. important."

Below that Danny signed each loose-leaf paper with the club password, a single word that meant attendance was mandatory, even after the biggest fight of their lives.

"*SMEGNY!*" the notes read.

Danny Spills the Beans

"Holy cow!" Lucas said, shifting his gaze nervously from side to side.

Danny had just finished telling him and Molly about the narrow escape from Mr. Sycamore, the secret room in the baseball-bat tower, and the dusty box of magic gum.

They were sitting in a tight circle under the oak tree, and Danny was holding the stick of Kosmic Kranberry in the palm of his hand. Danny's story was so mind-bendingly extraordinary that none of them could think of anything else to say, and they sat there for several minutes in silence.

"So you're telling me," Molly finally whispered, "that you hid in a closet in the study, and that closet was in fact a secret passageway, and at the end of that secret passageway was a secret room, and in that secret room you found this ancient gum, and that's what's making the Sluggers win?"

"I know it's hard to believe," Danny replied. "But I swear it's true."

He told them how he began to suspect the gum's power when little Thelonius Star hit a grand-slam home run while Danny chewed it the very night they got back from the mansion, and how Sam Slasky had turned a lion killer into a pussycat in the next game. When Tito Calagara flew around the bases like an Olympic sprinter, Danny was finally sure.

It had to be the gum!

Danny told them about the strange old books and the science equipment he had found on the table in the secret room, and how the box with the gum in it had been marked TESTING: LONGEST-LASTING KOSMIC KRANBERRY — MANCHESTER E. BODDLEBROOKS'S 53RD EXCITING FLAVOR.

"Think about it," Danny said. "It's the only explanation."

Molly stared into the distance.

Could it be true?

The Sluggers certainly had gone on an unprecedented roll ever since the three of them had gotten back from the old house. It just might be possible, she thought.

"Why didn't you tell us?" Lucas asked.

Danny looked down at the ground. He'd known Molly and Lucas for most of his life, and the three had shared a thousand secrets about a thousand different things. There was no real excuse.

"At first, I sort of forgot," Danny lied. How could he explain not wanting to let go of a secret he shared with a dead bubble-gum tycoon?

"Then when I realized what was going on, I thought you wouldn't believe me," he added. "And then . . . I guess I just got a little caught up in everything."

"I'll say," said Molly. Lucas took a deep breath.

"You know, it really isn't fair," Lucas said. "You got to be the most famous Sluggers fan in the world. All I got out of all this was six months of car-washing duty and a lifetime of piano lessons! I hope that's on your conscience."

Danny put the Kosmic Kranberry in his pocket carefully as a pair of joggers ran by.

"Danny, I just have one more question," Molly said after a minute. "If that gum is so magical, how come we've lost the last three games?"

Danny told her how he had saved four sticks of gum for the big series against the Tornadoes—one for every win the Sluggers needed to prevail. Everything was going perfectly until the Sluggers lost game three in Texas, even though Danny was chewing as hard as he could.

"I honestly don't understand how we lost that one," he said.

Lucas started doing the addition on his fingers. He was never very good at math either.

"So, what you're saying is . . . ," Lucas began.

"We've only got one stick left!" Molly finished the sentence.

Danny nodded.

Two games to win. One stick of magic gum. It was pretty easy to see the dilemma.

"We're doomed," Lucas said.

"Maybe," said Danny. "Maybe not."

EIGHTH INNING

Clubhouse Blues

Fifty-four hot dogs with everything are a lot to carry, but Danny could hardly feel the weight of the over-stuffed plastic bag as he walked into the Sluggers' locker room. He had finally told Molly and Lucas about his adventure at the Boddlebrooks mansion, and he felt as if an enormous burden had been lifted off his shoulders.

At least, one enormous burden had been lifted.

There was still the small matter of the Sluggers facing elimination against the most ferociously overpaid mercenaries in sporting history.

Danny walked around the clubhouse, handing out

two hot dogs to every man on the team. He had ordered them with extra sauerkraut since Canova wasn't pitching, but there was still plenty of onion goop to go around.

"Boy, am I glad to see you again," said Finchley Biggins with a sigh as Danny handed him his dogs. His eyes were heavy and he'd lost at least fifteen pounds from Diamond Bob's dirty water. He looked as if he had been to hell and back, not just Texas.

"What's the matter with everyone?" Danny asked quietly, looking around at the glum faces. It felt more like a funeral parlor than a locker room.

"What do you mean?" said Biggins.

"Well, don't you think the guys look a little down?" Danny whispered.

Biggins glanced around the room.

Boom-Boom Bigersley was sitting on a bench, a towel draped over his head. Sid Canova was muttering something to himself as he struggled to tie the laces on his shoes. Thelonius Star was pacing vacantly, his hands clasped behind his head.

This was how the Sluggers' locker room had looked for years, before they started winning.

"I hadn't noticed," Biggins said. "I guess we're just not looking forward to going out there. It's not much fun having your lunch handed to you in front of fifty-five thousand people, you know."

"But this is the biggest game of your lives!" Danny said to Biggins, his voice echoing in the quiet clubhouse.

Every major leaguer in the room turned his eyes toward Danny.

Danny froze, clutching the empty bag. He stood in the center of the room and looked up at the faces of the Sluggers players.

Planter and Minsky, Calagara and Mazoo, Sidewinder and Spagu.

"Uh," Danny stammered, "it's just . . . I mean . . . you've got to stop feeling sorry for yourselves."

Nobody said a word.

"You can't give up now," Danny went on. "You have a whole city behind you."

The Sluggers stared at him in silence, and Danny felt his heart sink. They'd never beat the Tornadoes like this, even with a piece of magic gum. The Sluggers were toast.

"You're my heroes," Danny said softly.

Finally, a low growl came from across the room.

"The kid is right!" said the voice, and everyone turned to see who it was.

Boom-Boom Bigersley was nearly motionless under the big white towel. Slowly he got up, pulling the towel off his head to reveal a pair of bloodshot eyes and a scowl that could have killed a cat.

"What have they got that we don't?" Bigersley said,

holding his hands out in front of him for emphasis. "Other than the big contracts and Hall of Fame careers, of course.

"Do they have our heart? Do they have our fans?" Bigersley asked. "Do they have a lucky eleven-year-old kid?"

"They got nothing!" yelled Mazoo, slamming his fist into his glove.

"I almost feel sorry for them!" said Biggins.

"I for one am tired of losing to those jerks, especially Barnworthy!" Bigersley shouted, looking around the room into his teammates' eyes.

"Yeah, you said it," said Chico Medley.

"So I tell you what. We're going to win tonight, and then we're going to win again tomorrow night," Bigersley shouted. "We just might win the World Series while we're at it!"

The Sluggers piled into the center of the room for high fives and cheers, smiles on their faces for the first time in days. Then, one by one, they headed out to the field, some still clutching their hot dogs.

When they were all gone, Danny stood alone in the locker room for a minute and caught his breath. He took the last piece of Kosmic Kranberry out of his pocket and stuck it in his mouth.

After all this time, he actually liked the taste.

All on the Field

It would be up to Vince Spagu and his remarkable knuckleball to salvage the Sluggers' chances of reaching their first World Series in 108 years.

"*It's do or die tonight,*" Wally Mandelberg said on the dugout monitor. "*This is going to be an epic battle.*"

"*Either that or a total blowout,*" said Bullet Santana.

Spagu took a deep breath and blew on his fingers to keep them warm. He kicked the dirt around the pitching rubber nervously. The crowd rose to its feet as Spagu took the sign from Medley, and Gus Schlays stepped into the box.

"*A big night for Vince,*" Mandelberg said. "*But part of him has got to be wishing he was back stacking groceries on a shelf. A lot less pressure.*"

Spagu's first pitch fluttered through the air like a moth and landed softly in the catcher's mitt.

The battle had begun.

Danny sat in the dugout, rubbing his hands together and rocking back and forth to keep warm. A cold mist was creeping over the field, hanging in damp wisps in the white beam of the stadium lights.

If the Tornadoes had expected the Sluggers to roll over for a fourth time in a row, they were getting a nasty surprise. The Sluggers scratched and clawed and scraped through the first four innings, playing as if their lives depended on it.

With the game scoreless and two men on in the second, Bruce Minsky ran down a fly ball to deep left field, catching it with his arms fully extended and his back to home plate. With the bases loaded and Barnworthy up in the third, Chuck Sidewinder dove to snare a shot down the third baseline, grabbing it inches off the ground.

Unfortunately for the Sluggers, the Tornadoes machine was running at full throttle too.

Tornadoes catcher Mungo McBust tumbled head-first into the Sluggers' dugout to catch a foul pop in the bottom of the fourth, emerging covered in sunflower seeds, with the ball held aloft.

"It might be a cold night, but these teams are hot," Santana said after the play. *"The pitching has been dynamite and the fielding even better."*

The Tornadoes had their second-best pitcher, a lefty named Rod Peckenpaw, on the mound. He had a small head and stocky legs, like a bowling pin with arms, and had once fought as a professional wrestler under the ring name the Executioner.

Every line-out, every strikeout, every pop-up, and every grounder produced a groan from the Sluggers faithful. One wrong move. One pitch left hanging over the plate. A single bobble in the infield and the Sluggers' season could be over.

Baseball is all about short-lived rallies and false buildups, and every inning of game six offered a new opportunity to live and die again. Younger fans covered their eyes and older ones popped antacid pills like peanuts.

As the night wore on, the temperature dropped and the fog grew thicker. By the time the Sluggers came to bat in the bottom of the sixth, the outfielders had almost disappeared in the mist.

"Weird weather, huh?" said Finchley Biggins, peering up the dugout steps.

Danny nodded. He was so nervous he'd barely noticed that his toes had gone completely numb and his fingers were like icicles.

"Okay, Tito, let's get something going," Biggins croaked as Calagara grabbed his bat and headed out onto the field. Danny started chewing the Kosmic Kranberry even harder. He hopped up onto one leg as Calagara swung.

"Base hit!" Mandelberg yelled as the ball shot into center field.

Spanky Mazoo followed with a shot of his own, and Calagara sprinted all the way to third.

"This is the Sluggers' best chance tonight," Santana

said. *"The question is, can Minsky put the bat on the ball."*

"He's got a .295 batting average against lefties," Mandelberg said. *"That's not too bad."*

Peckenpaw let out a roar of frustration as Minsky dug in at the batter's box.

"Grrrrrrrrrrrrrr!"

"That just might be the longest word Peckenpaw knows," Mandelberg chuckled.

"Not the sharpest tack on the board, you're right," Santana agreed. *"But he's not paid to think."*

Peckenpaw's first two bullets to Minsky were ninety-eight-mile-per-hour strikes, the first nearly grazing his knuckles, the second painting the outside corner of the plate. Minsky stepped out of the box and shook his head.

"Wow, those pitches were unhittable," said Santana.

"Minsky doesn't look like he wants to get back into the box any time soon," added Mandelberg. *"Two quick strikes and the boy's in a big hole."*

Peckenpaw held his glove up to his face to hide the ball, then went into his windup with a snarl.

Thump!

The pitch was even faster than the ones before, but it was right in Minsky's wheelhouse.

Winning Streak Stadium erupted as the ball shot

down the first baseline and rolled into the corner. The team poured out of the dugout as Calagara and Mazoo raced home.

"Two to nothing! Two to nothing! The Sluggers are on the board!" Mandelberg screamed. *"I've got goose bumps, my friend."*

"How about that!" said Santana. *"For the first time since they boarded the plane to Texas, the Sluggers look like their heads are in this series and they think they can win it!"*

The Tornadoes were furious. Le Swine kicked the watercooler in the visitors' dugout, and Peckenpaw slammed his glove down on the ground.

But his anger seemed to sharpen his concentration. The lefty struck out Star, Slasky, and Sidewinder on nine straight pitches to end the inning.

"The Tornadoes must have thought this was going to be a walkover after the disaster in Texas," Mandelberg said.

"It's all in Spagu's hands now," added Santana.

The former supermarket clerk held his ground. He got out of a bases-loaded jam in the seventh inning, and in the eighth he struck out center fielder Reggie Pinkowski, with the tying runs at second and third.

As Spagu took the mound to open the ninth, the crowd rose to its feet.

"Spa-gu! Spa-gu! Spa-gu!" they chanted.

Through the mist, Danny could pick out a banner shaped like a huge lemon: CHECKOUT TIME FOR TEXAS, it read.

"Wally, if the Sluggers can just hang on for one more inning, we may be back here tomorrow for something I know I never thought I'd see."

"Absolutely, Bullet: a deciding game seven at Winning Streak Stadium."

"Spagu looks unstoppable," Santana replied.

But his words were the kiss of death.

In the time it would take to say "Vince, there's a spill in aisle five," the knuckleballer's touch deserted him.

Gus Schlays led off with a double, and Spagu walked Riesling on four pitches in the dirt as the crowd howled in frustration.

"Looks like maybe you spoke too soon, Bullet," Mandelberg said. *"Rocco Barnworthy is coming to the plate. Nobody out. The tying runs are on base."*

"Biggins has Baxter Orejuela in the bullpen. I'd put him in now if I were the manager," Santana said. *"Spagu looks spent."*

"I think he's going to stick with him for one more batter, Bullet."

Crack!

A gasp rose from Winning Streak Stadium as the ball leapt off Barnworthy's bat. Fans covered their eyes and clutched their heads in despair. The gasp turned to a groan as the ball crashed into a billboard out past the center field wall.

"*That's gone!*" shouted Mandelberg. "*How about that? Schlays, Riesling, and Barnworthy are all coming around to score.*"

"*There goes the Sluggers' lead. There goes the game. There goes the season,*" Santana moaned as Barnworthy jumped on home plate in jubilation. "*The Tornadoes are up three to two.*"

Spagu stood in the middle of the infield, his eyes glazed over in shock. With a sigh, Finchley Biggins pulled down his cap and trudged out to the mound. Chico Medley trotted out to meet them.

On the dugout monitor, Danny could see the faces of the Sluggers fans, some streaked with tears. A mournful clap echoed through the stadium as Biggins patted Spagu on the back and the pitcher placed the ball in the manager's cupped hand.

"*What a rough way to end such a great performance,*" Mandelberg said. "*Spagu will be replaying that pitch to Barnworthy for the rest of his life.*"

"*Here comes Baxter Orejuela,*" Santana added. "*Let's hope he can stop the damage.*"

Orejuela did his job, setting down the Tornadoes with a barrage of fireballs.

"*Wally, Biggins must be kicking himself for not bringing his closer in earlier.*"

"The Sluggers have one last chance to save their season," Mandelberg said as the bottom of the ninth inning began.

"And what a season it has been," Santana added. *"But we'd need a miracle to save it now."*

Indeed they would.

Standing on the mound, shrouded by fog, was Magnus Ruffian. He was pitching in relief and on just two days' rest, and he wasn't happy about it.

"Ruffian looks even more intimidating in that mist, doesn't he, Bullet?" Mandelberg said.

"Certainly does," Santana replied. *"A brilliant move by Manager Le Swine—Ruffian looks downright insulted to be asked to come in as a relief pitcher, and an insulted Ruffian is not someone you want to face."*

A murmur of gloom spread through the Sluggers' dugout when Ruffian took the mound. This was bad news made much, much worse.

Danny chomped ferociously on the Kosmic Kranberry as Sam Slasky walked to the plate, shaking his fist nervously and muttering to himself.

"Patience, patience," Mandelberg urged. *"Don't just swing at anything."*

"Oh! That would have been a ball," Santana moaned as Slasky flung his bat at a pitch at his ankles, grounding it weakly to shortstop for the first out of the ninth.

"That's one nail in the coffin right there,"

Mandelberg said. *"Two outs to go. Here comes Thelonius Star."*

Ruffian growled at the diminutive right fielder, and Star growled right back.

"Yikes, Wally! A fastball right at Star's head."

"Look at the little guy," Mandelberg said as Star stepped back in the box. *"He's not going to let Ruffian rattle him."*

"Let's go already!" Ruffian screamed after Star reached out and nicked a fastball on the outside of the plate, barely staying alive. But Star wasn't going anywhere. The tiny right fielder fouled off eight straight pitches.

"That kid is a fighter. What guts! What heart!" said Santana.

In the Sluggers' dugout, the players stood riveted at the top of the steps, cheering their teammate on. If only Star could get on base, they'd have a chance.

Danny stretched the Kosmic Kranberry over his tongue and blew, making a bubble the size of a baseball.

"Come on, Star! Come on, Star!" he whispered to himself.

Ruffian went into his windup and fired, and this time Star made contact.

The crowd rose at once as the ball took off for center field.

"That one's got a chance," screamed Mandelberg.

"*It's way back. Pinkowski's at the wall. The ball is going, going . . .*"

"*It's caught,*" Santana groaned as Danny's bubble popped. "*Pinkowski's hauled it in right up against the wall, and there are two away.*"

"*That one sucked the air right out of here,*" Mandelberg said hopelessly. "*The Sluggers are down to their final out. This place is as dead as a morgue.*"

The Sluggers faithful were still standing, but most had buried their heads in their hands. They couldn't bear to look.

The only sound in the entire stadium was from the Tornadoes players shouting with glee. They were back in familiar territory, one out from the World Series. Even better, they'd be celebrating on the Sluggers' home field in front of their miserable fans.

Up in his luxury guest box above home plate, Diamond Bob chuckled as he popped open a bottle of champagne. Two hundred more bottles were hastily being put on ice in the visiting clubhouse.

"*Hey, look on the bright side,*" Santana said sadly. "*Spring training is just one hundred seventeen days away.*"

P. J. Planter was the last hope.

"*All Ruffian has to do is throw it down the middle of the plate,*" Mandelberg said. "*Planter hardly ever swings at the first pitch.*"

But the ruffian in Ruffian got the better of him. The first pitch was a bullet, but straight at Planter's head.

A groan spread through the stadium as the ball crashed into his helmet with a thud, sending Planter sprawling to the ground.

"That was a terrible time to do that," said Santana. *"He's put the tying run on first and brought the winning run to bat."*

"Get up, punk!" yelled Ruffian, stalking toward the plate.

Planter wobbled to one knee, then stood swaying in the batter's box.

The stadium shook as the crowd stomped its feet and Planter staggered to first base.

In the dugout, Boom-Boom Bigersley grabbed his bat.

"One more time, kid," he said as he passed Danny, holding out his Louisville Slugger for good luck.

Danny waved the Kosmic Kranberry over the bat, and Bigersley turned and winked at him as he climbed the dugout steps.

The fog was so thick now that Bigersley could barely find the batter's box. He waved his bat in front of him like a Spanish explorer hacking a path through a rain forest.

"These are no conditions for baseball," Mandelberg said. *"It's spooky."*

"*I keep thinking I'm going to see Sherlock Holmes or Captain Hook walking in from center field,*" added Santana.

"Come on!" Ruffian screamed, loud enough for everyone in the stadium to hear. "Let's finish it!"

Danny squeezed his eyes closed.

"*It's all on the line,*" Mandelberg said. "*Can this crowd get any wilder?*"

As Ruffian reached back into his windup, the screams turned to silence.

Bigersley swung at the pitch with all his might and shot off toward first base as fast as his legs could carry him.

"*Oh no! A pop-up,*" Mandelberg groaned. "*That's it. It's over.*"

"*Yeah, but what a pop-up,*" Santana replied slowly. "*Where has it gone?*"

Up, up, up the ball went into the night.

It soared out beyond the upper deck and up past the stadium lights into the thickest part of the clouds. Bigersley glanced up at the sky as he rounded first and kept running.

All six Tornadoes infielders rushed into the center of the field, waiting for the ball to come down. They pointed and gestured at the sky as Bigersley scampered to second and Planter lurched to third.

"*Where's that ball?*" Santana yelled. The crowd

craned their necks toward the sky. The Sluggers ran out of the dugout and stared upward.

Danny opened his eyes and followed them onto the field.

As Bigersley reached third base, the crowd began to murmur, and when he turned the corner, the murmur became a rumble. Planter crossed home plate, collapsed on the ground, and stared up into the clouds.

"Run, Boom-Boom!" the crowd shouted. "Run!"

Suddenly, Danny saw a white object whistling out of the mist. It was picking up speed as it shot down toward the Tornadoes players.

"I got it!" screamed McBust.

"It's mine!" shouted Ruffian.

"My ball! My ball!" yelled Riesling as Bigersley shot past him down the line toward home plate, his arms pumping.

Ruffian pushed his teammates away, planted his feet firmly on the ground, and reached his glove up over his head. If he made the catch, the Sluggers' season would be over, but the ball was traveling way too fast for that.

It smashed through the webbing of Ruffian's glove and continued straight through, plunking him on the head and knocking him out cold.

The ball came to rest just a foot in front of home plate as Bigersley slid in.

"I cannot believe what I just saw!" Mandelberg screamed. *"We asked for a miracle and we got one!"*

"The Sluggers win!" Santana yelled. *"Four to three. Hug me, Wally!"*

"The Sluggers are still alive. We're going to game seven!" Mandelberg said.

As Bigersley leapt into the arms of Danny and his teammates, the shocked Tornadoes clustered around the unconscious Ruffian.

He was the only person in America who would have no recollection whatsoever of the Magnificent Mist Miracle of Game Six.

The Last Resort

"No way!" Molly said when Danny cornered her and Lucas outside school the next morning.

"Not on your life!" Lucas shook his head emphatically. "I'd do anything for you, man. Except that."

"But it's the only way!" Danny protested. "And he's not that creepy."

"Danny, if a nine-thousand-year-old man with bugged-out eyes living in a creaky old mansion isn't creepy, what is?" Molly said. "If you look up 'creepy' in the dictionary, it says 'Mr. Sycamore.'"

Danny had to admit he'd had more than one

nightmare in the past few weeks that ended with a vision of Mr. Sycamore's wobbly eye staring at him through the closet keyhole, and he shuddered every time he recollected the bang of the old man's cane coming down the corridor outside the study.

But game seven was just eleven hours away, and he needed a stick of gum!

Diamond Bob was probably plotting ways to crush the Sluggers at that very minute.

"I'm going," said Danny. "Right after school."

"You've got to be out of your mind," Molly whispered, grabbing Danny by the arm. "What if Mr. Sycamore knows you took the gum? He certainly has to know by now that you snuck into that study."

Lucas grabbed Danny's other arm.

"You know in the movies when the criminal returns to the scene of the crime?" he said. "You ever notice how it doesn't work out too well for him?"

"This is different," Danny said.

"Can you even comprehend what kind of trouble you're going to get into with your parents?" Lucas said. "This is like burn-the-house-down kind of trouble!"

"They don't have to know all the details," Danny said. "Anyway, there's no sense us all getting into trouble. I'll go alone."

"If I got caught again, Danny . . ." Lucas shook his head. "I'll be taking tuba lessons next."

Molly looked at Danny with a mix of concern and curiosity.

"Let's just suppose you went," she said after a minute. "How do you plan to get out to West Bubble anyway?"

"Yeah, are you going to take your bike on the freeway at night?" Lucas asked. "Even you couldn't be that crazy!"

Danny rubbed his hands together. He turned his gaze from one friend to the other.

"Er, that's where you guys come in," he said slowly. "How much money have you got?"

Final Preparations

Danny was out of his seat at school the moment the last bell rang. He jogged all the way home, bounded up the stairs of his building, and made a beeline for his bedroom.

All told, he had seventeen dollars in allowance money stored away in an antique metal bank shaped like an old-time baseball player. Not bad, Danny thought, though his mind did race back to the gazillions Diamond Bob had offered him to root for the Tornadoes.

He was halfway out the door when the phone rang.

"Have I got news for you!" said Harold Gurkin when Danny picked up the phone. "We're all going to be in the mayor's box tonight—your mother, Max, and me! We'll be right behind you."

"You will?" Danny said. His heart dropped.

"Yeah," his father said. "We can cheer for you every time you pop out of the dugout! Isn't that great?"

Danny had figured with his parents watching the game at home, they might not notice his absence for four or five innings. Now he had to come up with an excuse in a hurry.

"The thing is, Dad, you might not see as much of me as you would imagine," Danny said slowly, his fingers gripping the receiver nervously.

"What do you mean?" Harold said.

"I'll probably be in the clubhouse a lot. In fact, I might not be out on the field at all," he said.

"Not on the field?" said Harold. "But you're the ball boy."

Danny gulped.

"Right, that's true, but then there is the Curse of the Poisoned Pretzel to consider," Danny said.

"What does that have to do with it?"

"Well, you see, a lot of the guys are afraid that with this being game seven, the ghost of Manchester Boddlebrooks might walk the clubhouse unless there are some good vibes there," Danny said.

"Really? Gosh, that sounds serious," his father laughed. "Just make sure no bubble-gum tycoon's ghost falls over on you! I guess we'll come and find you after the game, then. Go, Sluggers!"

"Sure thing!" Danny said. "See you later."

Pretty good for a spur-of-the-moment story, Danny thought with relief. He ran out the front door, taking the stairs two at a time.

There wasn't a minute to spare.

Danny's first stop was Willie's stand. The hot-dog man was talking to some early customers, and they were all waving their hands in the air like baseball players frantically trying to spot a pop-up in the mist.

"What a game!" Willie said, shaking Danny by the shoulders. "It was like magic."

"Unbelievable," Danny agreed. "Best game ever, no doubt about it."

"I can hardly take it again tonight," Willie said. "I hope I have enough hot dogs."

Danny bought six hot dogs with everything, both for good luck and in case he got hungry on the trip.

"Why aren't you buying dogs for the whole team?" Willie asked.

"Oh, ah, I've got something to do first," Danny said. "Molly and Lucas will be over later to pick up the team dogs."

Willie's assistant handed Danny his order, and he

274

raced off toward the basketball courts at Quincy Park. It was 4:51, just two hours until the first pitch of the most important game of all time.

The park was just filling up with kids, and they were all talking about the game. Everywhere Danny looked, children were waving their hands in the air in mock confusion, then throwing themselves on the ground in slapstick imitations of Magnus Ruffian getting conked on the head.

Danny leaned against the fence and waited for Molly and Lucas to arrive. Finally, he heard the patter of footsteps.

"Hey, man," Lucas said breathlessly, shoving a wad of bills and coins into Danny's hand. "Take it all. That's everything."

"Great," Danny said. "How much is here?"

"Four dollars and thirty-eight cents," Lucas said, rubbing his nose.

"Four dollars!" Danny yelled. "And thirty-eight cents! That's it?"

"Sorry," Lucas said. "I spent most of my money on hot dogs this year."

"Oh, man!"

Danny needed more money. By the time Molly arrived, it was nearly five-thirty and Danny was beside himself. He had a lot to do before game time.

"My father told me this money was only to be used

in a major emergency," she said nervously, holding the bills tightly in her hand.

"Well, that sounds like what this is," Danny said impatiently, grabbing the money and counting it quickly.

"Wow," he said. "There's a hundred bucks here!"

"Yeah, I know," said Molly, biting her bottom lip. "Danny, are you sure about this? I could come with you if you want."

Danny thrust the bills into his pants pocket and grabbed the bag of hot dogs off the ground.

"No," he said. "Anyway, you guys have to take care of everything else."

Danny reached into his pocket and grabbed a note he had hurriedly scribbled during Mrs. Sherman's class while she was barking out a long explanation of the history of the stocks as a way to punish children in medieval Europe.

It was a wonder she hadn't discovered him.

The note said "MANAGER BIGGINS, READ THIS!" on the front, and inside it explained that Danny was on an important mission to fetch the oldest Sluggers fan in the world and there was no reason to panic. He was sending his friends in his place.

"The team car picks us up at six o'clock at Willie's stand, right?" Molly said.

"And it's fifty-six hot dogs?" Lucas asked.

"Yeah, with everything and extra onions," said Danny. "Just ask Willie. They'll be on the house."

Molly and Lucas nodded.

"Okay, then," Danny said, tapping fists with each of them. "I'll see you after the game."

You're Danny Gurkin!

Danny had never hailed a cab on his own before, and he wasn't sure how to do it. Would they even stop for a kid?

He stood on the corner of Splotnick Street in the waning afternoon sun and put his hand in the air.

Screech!

"That was easy," Danny thought as he hopped into the back of the car.

"Where you goin', buddy?" asked the driver, pulling the taxi into heavy traffic without so much as a glance. There was a chorus of honks and curses as cars swerved to get out of the way.

"Uh, West Bubble, please," Danny said politely, and was surprised how quickly his body shot forward into the Plexiglas that separated him from the front seat when the cabbie slammed on the brakes.

"*West Bubble?*" said the driver, turning around. "That's got to be thirty miles from here! Do you have any idea how much that's going to cost, kid?"

Danny pulled the wad of bills out of his pocket and held it up to the glass. The taxi shot off down the street.

It wasn't until several minutes later, after the car had jolted to a stop at a traffic light, that the driver turned around again.

"Hey, you're that kid that does all the crazy stuff with the hot dogs!" said the cabbie. Danny noticed a plastic figurine glued to the dashboard that looked just like Sid Canova. "You're Danny Gurkin!"

Danny nodded.

"What're you going out to West Bubble for?" the taxi driver asked. "The game starts in ninety minutes!"

Danny didn't know what to say. He certainly wasn't going to tell the cabbie he was on a desperate quest for more magic gum!

"Official Sluggers business," Danny said. "I'm not allowed to talk about it."

"Wow!" said the driver as they shot across two lanes of traffic to barely make the turn onto the Harry Tinkleford Highway. "I thought you'd lost your touch there for a while, but you really came through last night. What a game, huh?"

The cabbie started waving his hands in the air to show he'd seen the final play. Danny hoped he was steering with his knees.

"Yep, it was," Danny said, clutching the seat to keep

his balance. He was starting to feel queasy. "It's a good thing I haven't eaten those hot dogs yet," he thought.

"Seeing Ruffian out cold like that," mused the cabbie, cutting off a Volkswagen and honking his horn. "That was beautiful! Am I right or what?"

"I'm sorry," Danny said. "I'm a little preoccupied. How long is it going to take to get there?"

The driver looked back at Danny through the rearview mirror.

"Oh, I didn't realize you were in a hurry." He smiled, pushing down on the accelerator and shooting into the fast lane. "I'll have you there in a jiffy."

NINTH INNING

Taxi Ride

It was just getting dark by the time the taxi pulled into the gravel driveway at Manchester Boddlebrooks's West Bubble estate, and the moon was still low in the sky, giving the hedges that lined the road an eerie bluish glow.

"Are you sure this is where you're going?" the cab-driver said nervously.

"Yeah, this is it," Danny said. He glanced at his watch. It was nearly six-thirty.

The gravel drive was just wide enough for the car to squeeze through, and the overgrown hedges brushed noisily against the roof and windows as the taxi rumbled past.

"This is going to cost you extra," the driver said. "This car's a rental."

Finally, the driveway opened up and the mansion came into view.

"Whoa!" said the cabbie. "What the heck is that?"

Danny looked up at the darkened mansion. The house was imposing in the daytime. In the early-evening gloom, it was downright medieval. The baseball-bat towers cast dark shadows on the front lawn, and the dozens of round baseball windows in the upper floors looked like hollow eyes. Danny wished he had taken Molly up on her offer to come with him.

The car pulled around to the enormous hot-dog front doors.

"This place is spooky," the driver said slowly, glancing up at the mansion's cracked stone walls.

The taxi meter read $63.75, and Danny reached into his pocket for the money.

"I can't leave a kid alone in a place like this. I'd get arrested," said the cabbie. "I'll wait."

"But I don't have enough money for that," Danny said.

"That's all right," said the driver. "I think the story will be payment enough. Wait till I tell the guys down at the depot about this!"

"Who are you meeting here anyway?" the cabbie asked.

"Um, my grandfather," Danny lied. He opened the taxi door, grabbed his bag of hot dogs, and walked slowly toward the front of the mansion.

Just the thought of what Mr. Sycamore might look like at night made Danny shudder. What if he was angry? What if he was *really* angry? What if he was eye-rattlingly, cane-shakingly furious?

Danny hadn't exactly thought through how he would sneak back into the secret round room and grab the Kosmic Kranberry, or what he would say to Mr. Sycamore. His heart was pounding.

Slowly, he reached up for one of the door's heavy iron knockers.

"Maybe I should just go home," Danny thought as his fingers grasped the cold metal handle. No sooner had he touched it than the enormous door swung back with a terrifying creak, and a thin voice hissed out at him from the darkness.

"I've been expecting you," it said.

The Inner Sanctum

"Come in! Come in!" said Mr. Sycamore, pulling Danny into the grand front hallway and slamming the door closed behind him. He flipped a light switch on the wall.

"B-but . . . ," Danny stuttered, his eyes adjusting to the dim glow of the chandelier. "How did you know I was out there?"

"Oh, I heard the car," the old man said quickly, leaning on his wooden cane and fixing his good eye on Danny's face. "And as I said, I figured you'd be back at some point."

Mr. Sycamore's other eye darted up to the oil painting of Manchester Boddlebrooks that hung on the wall behind Danny's head, then shot down to the bag of hot dogs in his visitor's hands.

"Oh, good, you brought something to eat," Mr. Sycamore said. "I'm famished."

Danny looked around the room. It seemed to have been dusted and polished since he was last there, and there was a sign sitting on the table in front of the wide double door:

BODDLEBROOKS MANSION *UNDER RENOVATION.*
GRAND REOPENING SOON!
PLEASE BEAR WITH US.

"We're fixing up everything, right down to the wooden bench in Benchwarmer Banana," Mr. Sycamore explained when he saw that Danny was staring at the notice. "You've made an old man very happy.

You and that wonderful Mr. Frompovich."

Danny couldn't believe it. The mayor had actually come through!

Mr. Sycamore turned quickly toward the other end of the hall, his cane thudding on the floor as he walked. When he reached the double door, he spun around. Danny was still standing by the front door, frozen on the spot.

"Well, aren't you coming?" Mr. Sycamore said impatiently. "The game starts in twenty minutes!"

The old man led the way down the corridor, and Danny walked slowly after him, amazed at what a little wax and a fresh coat of paint could do.

Mr. Sycamore opened the door to a warm, cozy room that Danny was sure he hadn't seen on his first visit to the house. Half the room was set up as a bedroom, with a single four-poster bed and two bedside tables covered in old black-and-white photographs.

At the other end of the room was a Persian carpet. There was a watermelon red sofa and a small coffee table on one side, and a large old-fashioned television on the other, which emitted a hissing noise and a scratchy black-and-white image. Danny was surprised it was working at all.

"These are my living quarters," Mr. Sycamore said. "What do you think?"

"Nice," said Danny.

"I can't be jumping around from bedroom to bedroom like Manchester used to do," he chuckled.

Danny grinned nervously.

"Sit down, sit down," the old man said. "We've got a lot to discuss before the game."

The game!

There were just minutes left until the first pitch and Danny still didn't have any Kosmic Kranberry. There was no time for tricks. He'd have to come clean and hope maybe the old man would let him have just one more stick. He was a Sluggers fan, after all, and once he realized what powers the gum had, he'd have to agree.

"Uh, about the game, Mr. Sycamore," Danny said slowly. "The last time I was here, I um, well, I found something . . ."

Mr. Sycamore stared at Danny but didn't say a word.

". . . in the study . . . ," Danny continued.

He was so nervous his hands were shaking, but he went on.

"It was something . . . amazing. Something . . . extraordinary," Danny said. "It was . . ."

"Really horrible-tasting gum?" Mr. Sycamore said, his milky eye darting around the room like a firefly.

Danny's jaw dropped.

"You mean you know about the gum?" Danny said.

"Well, of course I know about the gum," Sycamore

replied. "And I also knew you would take some."

"You knew?" Danny asked.

"I had an idea you'd try the second you and your friends showed up here," Mr. Sycamore chuckled. "And then of course I saw you through the keyhole."

Danny felt his face redden.

"You saw me!" he said. "How come you didn't say anything?"

"It's not every day you come across a Sluggers fan who still has hope after 108 years of losing," Sycamore said. "That gum has been waiting for someone like you to find it for a very long time. I figured I shouldn't stand in the way."

"But, Mr. Sycamore," Danny said. "I don't understand."

The black-and-white television over Seymour Sycamore's shoulder crackled softly with the Sluggers pregame show, but the old man seemed unaware of it. He sat down on the red couch and gestured for Danny to join him.

"I guess I ought to start at the beginning," he said.

The Story of Seymour Sycamore

Even after he became a fantastically rich man, Manchester Boddlebrooks liked to wander down from his gleaming red mansion to watch the children play baseball in West Rock Park.

A man of such vast wealth walked slowly in those days, to make clear that he was never in a hurry. Manchester carried a cane, just for effect, and he had already started wearing the dazzling white suits for which he would later be famous. He put on weight in a manner considered compulsory for a man of his financial stature, though he had not yet reached the giant girth of his later years.

On sunny Saturday mornings, the bubble-gum tycoon would take a seat on a park bench behind the baseball diamond, unfurl his newspaper, and reminisce about his days as a groundskeeper.

As he watched the kids play, he would indulge in a running daydream that he would one day buy his very own major-league team. It would be the greatest team of all time, winning championships every year as simply as blowing a bubble.

Manchester Mastications, Inc., had already come up with dozens of exciting bubble-gum flavors, and they were churning out a new one every three months. It wouldn't be long until he had enough money to build a stadium.

One Saturday morning in early May when Manchester was at the park, his eye was caught by a talented eleven-year-old shortstop who sucked up every ball hit to him like a vacuum. Actually, the first motorized vacuum cleaner would not be invented for another couple of years, and that was a ghastly contraption that required a long rubber hose, a large tank of gasoline, and a horse. Still, the kid was good.

"What do they call you, son?" Manchester asked when the teams changed sides between innings.

"The name's Smegny," said the boy. "Lou Smegny."

Manchester looked the boy up and down. He was wearing a torn baseball jersey and a dirty cap, and his glove was practically as old as he was. It looked as if he'd stitched it together himself to keep it from falling apart.

"Smegny . . . Smegny . . . ," Manchester said, trying to recall the name. "Doesn't your father work down at the docks?"

"Yes, sir," said the boy. "Actually, my pop does all sorts of things to get by."

"Of course he does," Manchester said. "He's a good man."

Smegny turned to go back to the game, but Manchester stopped him. He had an idea.

"Lou, how'd you like to come work for me?" said the bubble-gum tycoon. "You can start by coming to the factory after school; then we can find more steady work when you get older."

The boy shrugged. Times were tough back then,

288

and people didn't turn down work, not even eleven-year-olds.

"Sure," said Smegny.

"We have a little ball club down at the factory," said Manchester. "Would you like to be on it?"

"Yeah," said Smegny. "Super."

As the boy grew, his baseball talents increased, and he proved to be just as good a worker. He started off delivering gum after school, but moved up quickly. By the time he was fifteen, young Lou Smegny was in charge of inventory for all of Manchester Mastications, and at seventeen, Boddlebrooks made him vice president of new flavors.

Manchester and Smegny spent hours in the lab in the baseball-bat tower where Boddlebrooks worked on his secret new concoctions, decanting beakers of boiled-down fruit syrup into jars of rubbery goo. The two of them perfected Simply Sauerkraut, Victory Vanilla, and Patently Peanut Shell in a single month.

The following year, Manchester had saved up enough money to build a stadium in town and to start up his very own big-league ball club. He called the team the Sluggers because he thought it sounded nice.

In the early days, many of the players were drafted straight off the company pickup team. Back then, ballplayers didn't earn the big bucks they do today, and most had to work other jobs to make ends meet. Smegny was the Sluggers' star shortstop, but he continued to work down at the factory.

Manchester had become one of the wealthiest men in the country by then, with assembly lines pumping out fifty-two different bubble-gum flavors, each one more popular than the last.

But the tycoon wasn't satisfied. He was convinced there was one more flavor out there, and he thought about it night and day.

As a little boy in the old country, Manchester had been crazy about a small red fruit called the lingonberry that the village grocer sold for next to nothing in a brown paper bag. They were as sour as the czar of Russia and just as reviled.

"Disgusting," his friends said.

"Filthy," his grandmother snapped.

"Repulsive," his younger brother belched.

Young Manchester didn't listen to any of them. He carried the berries around with him wherever he went. As a matter of fact, he had just run out of them on the day his parents died—the day he decided that he and his brother would immigrate to America.

"Ah, how I miss the simple tartness of that great fruit," Manchester groaned from behind the desk at the plush executive office of Manchester Mastications. "America is a wonderful country, but it is missing this one important thing."

"I don't know lint from lingonberries," Smegny admitted when Boddlebrooks told him about the fruit. "But they sound a lot like cranberries."

"Cranberries?" Manchester asked, raising his eyebrows.

"I think they grow up north," Smegny went on. "I never cared much for them myself. Sour as all hell! People eat them at Thanksgiving."

The bubble-gum tycoon sat up in his leather seat, his eyes twinkling with excitement.

"Can you get me some, Lou?" Manchester asked. "They need to be right from the source. As fresh as possible."

"Whatever you say, boss," Smegny replied. "But it'll take a while."

It was no small thing to head north in those days. There were horses to prepare and lodging to arrange. Smegny did not return for several weeks.

While he was gone, Manchester continued to pore over the old books he had brought with him from his homeland. Books on food and fortune. Books on fate and the universe. Books full of potions and ancient recipes.

Smegny's travels took him to every cranberry bog in the Northeast, and to the frozen lands above.

When he finally returned, Smegny had a bushel of cranberries under each arm and a wagonful of the tart fruit in a carriage out front. Strapped to the roof was the longest canoe Manchester had ever seen, and sticking out the window was an old-fashioned fishing rod.

"What's that smell?" Manchester said after the two men shook hands.

Smegny thought for a moment. Then he pulled a crumpled-up paper bag out of his jacket pocket and held it up to his boss.

"Must be these fish sticks," he said. "Some locals up north gave them to me."

Manchester helped Smegny carry the cranberries in from the carriage, and the two men went straight to the lab. They worked around the clock for weeks until finally Manchester was satisfied.

"This is it!" the bubble-gum tycoon cried out late

one evening, a beaker of concentrated cranberry syrup in his hands. "Try that. It's delicious."

He handed the beaker to Smegny, who took one sip and nearly spat it out.

"But this is awful," he said, wiping his mouth. "It

tastes even worse than Simply Sauerkraut."

"Maybe it could do with a bit more sugar," Boddle-brooks conceded. "I'll tell you what, you concentrate on baseball and I'll keep tinkering."

The Sluggers had fallen back in the standings while Smegny was away. Now they started to play a bit better.

Each day, the shortstop would take Manchester's latest cranberry concoction to the ballpark and chew it during the game to see if the bubble-gum tycoon's fine-tuning was helping the taste. It wasn't, but Smegny owed everything to the giant bubble-gum tycoon, and he didn't want to be rude.

As the season wore on and the Sluggers rose in the standings, Boddlebrooks became more and more convinced that his Old World books were right. Whether they were lingonberries or cranberries, there was more to them than their controversial taste.

The better the team played, the more sure Boddle-brooks was. He cornered Smegny in the locker room after the Sluggers beat the Charleston Bruisers 19–3 and moved into first place.

"Lou, let me ask you something," Manchester whispered. "When you're chewing the cranberry gum, does anything strange happen?"

"What, you mean besides feeling nauseous?"

Smegny laughed. "I've been meaning to tell you, boss. I think that gum needs more work. It's still way too sour."

"No! No!" said Boddlebrooks. "I think it's perfect. It's more than perfect. In fact, I think the gum is behind everything!"

Smegny looked confused.

"What do you mean, the gum?" he said, taking a seat on the bench and pulling off his cleats.

"The cranberries. Don't you see?" Boddlebrooks said excitedly, sitting down next to him, his eyes shifting from side to side. "They're different. They're . . . lucky."

"What are you talking about, boss?" Smegny asked skeptically.

"Lou, I've been looking into it. You've got to read more if you're ever going to learn anything," Boddle-brooks huffed.

He told Smegny about the thousands of years of calamity that went into producing a single cranberry. The ice ages and mass extinctions necessary to create the perfect growing conditions. The centuries of rot and decay.

"They're just like lingonberries," Boddlebrooks whispered, a faraway look in his eyes. "Since I was a boy I've always known there was something about them. It's all in the books."

What he was saying might have seemed crazy to

some people, but Manchester had seen much stranger things as a child growing up in his native country. In the Old World, there were miracles and there was misfortune, and nobody doubted for a minute that the two could be controlled. How else to explain why some elephants could learn to swing on a trapeze and some simply could not?

Smegny looked his boss in the eye. There was no doubt the team had been on a roll since he'd come back from the North, but Smegny chalked that up to his stellar play at shortstop, not the gum. Still, Manchester Boddlebrooks was the greatest man Smegny had ever known, and he had never seen him more convinced of anything in his life. Perhaps there was something about the Kosmic Kranberry.

"So, what do we do?" Smegny said.

Boddlebrooks put his hand on his young friend's shoulder and smiled.

"Just keep chewing, Lou," he said. "Just keep chewing."

Fingers Crossed

"So that's what I did," the old man told Danny, leaning back on the couch. "I kept chewing that awful gum for the rest of the season."

There was a long pause. Danny stared at Mr. Sycamore, his eyes nearly popping out of his head.

"You're Lou Smegny?"

"Well, I was," Mr. Sycamore replied.

The old man explained how he disappeared following the championship season, his body crippled by the tumbling bubble-gum tycoon and his mind a blank slate. If it hadn't been for the name tag on his hospital bed, he would not even have known his name.

The young shortstop lay in the hospital for a week, and every night he had the same vivid dream. He was sitting in the glow of a warm fire in a cozy igloo, a bowl of delicious fish sticks in his hand.

He checked out of the hospital and headed for Canada.

Mr. Sycamore told Danny about his days with the Nabutee, a tribe he had first come across when he drove too far north during his search for cranberries, and how he had taken the name Seeyamoora.

"I decided to shorten it to Seymour when I came back," Mr. Sycamore explained, recalling his 1934 confrontation with Skidmore Boddlebrooks in front of the great mansion. "It was a spur-of-the-moment kind of thing."

"What *did* make you come back?" Danny asked.

"Well, it's a bit boring up there," Mr. Sycamore said. "Except for the fish sticks. Darned tasty, I must say. But after thirty-six years, you get a little tired of them.

"Actually, if it hadn't been for the Great Thaw I'd probably still be up there," Mr. Sycamore mused.

"The Great Thaw?" Danny asked.

"One day in the spring of 1934, the sun came out and it didn't go away," Sycamore explained. "The snow began to melt, and the igloos started to droop.

"I was patching up a corner of my little home that had melted away when I noticed something in the ice deep under my feet," the old man told Danny. "I grabbed my pick and dug down to it, and found something I hadn't seen for decades."

It was the brown cardboard box he had been carrying when he arrived, and it was filled with Kosmic Kranberry.

"One taste of that gum and everything started to flood back," Sycamore said. "Two weeks later, I packed my few belongings into a little suitcase, said goodbye to my Nabutee friends, and headed south."

"But . . . ," Danny said finally. "If you're Smegny, that would make you, like, more than a hundred years old!"

"One hundred and twenty-six, to be precise," Mr. Sycamore said proudly. "I know I don't look it."

"But that's impossible!" Danny exclaimed. "You should be . . ."

"Dead?" Mr. Sycamore said. "Well, it's a funny

thing about cranberries. They taste awful, but if kept in a very cold environment and eaten in great quantities, they're extremely good for you. Keep the arteries from clogging up, or so I'm told."

Danny was speechless.

"I only wish they did something for my cataracts." Sycamore shrugged, his milky eye shooting off toward the ceiling.

Suddenly, there was a loud thumping at the front door.

The taxi driver!

Danny looked at his watch. It was two minutes to seven.

"Mr. Sycamore," Danny said. "Quick, the game starts in five minutes! We need more gum!"

Seymour Sycamore stared straight into Danny's eyes. For the first time, his wandering pupil was at rest.

"But, my dear boy, there's no need for the gum anymore," said the old man.

Danny was confused. Of course they needed the gum!

"But this is it! It's game seven!" Danny cried. "We can't lose now."

"Son, the Sluggers aren't winning because of the gum!" Mr. Sycamore said. "They're winning because of you!"

Danny furrowed his brow. What was the old man talking about? He had been rooting for the Sluggers all his life, but the team had only started winning since he found the Kosmic Kranberry.

The volume was turned down on the old television set, but Danny could see Sid Canova taking his warmup pitches.

The banging from outside was growing louder and louder.

"Who in the world could that be?" Mr. Sycamore said, getting up and shuffling out of the room. He returned a minute later with a very nervous-looking taxi driver trailing behind him.

"*This* is your grandfather?" the cabbie said, giving Danny an anxious glance.

"Yeah," Danny replied. "Sort of."

"I'm Lenny," said the driver, extending his hand to Mr. Sycamore. "Lenny Pobjoy. Kid, what's up? I've been out there for half an hour. You coming?"

"Oh, you can't go now," Mr. Sycamore said. "The game's about to start. Make yourself comfortable. You'll have to watch it here."

The driver looked from Danny to Mr. Sycamore and back. He ran his hand through his hair.

"Well, I guess nobody will be looking for a taxi now, especially not all the way out here," he said, glancing over at the television. "Don't mind if I do.

"Let me see if I can get a better picture on that old set of yours," said the cabbie.

Danny pulled Mr. Sycamore to one side.

"What do you mean they're winning because of me?" he whispered.

"What do you think?" Mr. Sycamore replied. "That the cranberries do everything? If cranberries were that powerful, why would they be stuck out in smelly marshes?"

"But isn't the gum magic?"

"Oh, it's magic all right," said the old man. "But I've always believed it has as much to do with who's chewing it. It has to be a die-hard, a true believer. The kind of fan who only comes along once in a generation."

Mr. Sycamore smiled at Danny.

"Someone like me," he said. "Or someone like you. Anyway, the gum's already done its part."

"But I don't understand," Danny said.

"It's a bit like those tugboats down at the docks where my father worked," Mr. Sycamore explained. "They helped get the big ships out to sea, but once they got past the sound they were on their own.

"It's up to us now. There isn't a fan out there that doesn't think we can win tonight. There isn't a player on the team who isn't convinced he's going to the World

Series. That's more powerful than all the Kosmic Kranberry in the world, if you ask me."

"What a great night for baseball, my friends! A perfect night for baseball."

Wally Mandelberg's voice burst out of the television set as Lenny Pobjoy fiddled with the volume. The Sluggers were whipping the ball around the infield.

"You got a beer?" the taxi driver said.

"I'm afraid not," Mr. Sycamore replied. "I do have some popcorn if you want, but it's a little stale."

The old man turned to Danny.

"So! You're the boy with all the superstitions," he said. "What should we do now?"

Danny looked around the room. There wasn't much time.

"Well, first we have to close all the windows," Danny began. "And, uh, I've actually got some hot dogs with everything in the bag over there. There's extra onion goop because Canova's on the mound."

"Of course," said the old man. "That makes perfect sense."

Mr. Sycamore and Lenny Pobjoy scurried around the room closing all the windows, while Danny tore open the bag of hot dogs. There were two for each of them.

"Sorry," he said. "They're cold, but they'll still do the trick."

Mr. Sycamore turned to Danny.

"There's still time to run and get the gum if you want," he said.

Danny paused for a second.

"That's okay," he replied. "I think we'll be fine without it. The most important thing is to be in position for the first pitch."

The three fans squeezed in together on the sofa just as the television camera showed an overhead shot of a packed Winning Streak Stadium, the grass glowing in the bright lights.

"I really like our chances tonight," Lenny said. "What about you?"

"We'll have to pull out all the stops if we want to beat the Tornadoes," Danny said. "Do you know how to cross your toes?"

The camera panned down the Sluggers bench. Sitting in the dugout, on either side of Finchley Biggins, were Molly and Lucas, each of them screaming their lungs out.

In the box seats right behind the dugout were Harold, Lydia, and Max Gurkin, all stuffing heaping hot dogs with everything into their mouths. Mayor Fred Frompovich was making a victory sign in the row behind them.

Sid Canova placed his foot on the pitching rubber and Winning Streak Stadium rose to its feet. The rookie

leaned in for the sign from Chico Medley, cradling the ball behind his back.

In the flicker of an ancient television set that had never before broadcast a Sluggers game seven, Danny Gurkin, Seymour Sycamore, and Lenny Pobjoy crossed their legs one by one. As the first pitch flew from Canova's hand, the three fans sucked in a long, deep breath and held it for good luck.

ACKNOWLEDGMENTS

Firstly, I must thank Suzy Capozzi and Kate Klimo, my editor and my publisher, without whose enthusiasm and support this book would have remained a ten-page writing-class submission. I am hugely grateful as well to Vicky Burnett, my wife and unofficial editor, for countless hours spent poring over drafts, debating the plot, and preserving my sanity — often at the expense of her own.

I am also indebted to Zoe Pagnamenta, my wonderful agent and great friend. Finally, thanks to my parents, Susan and Mark Haven, who instilled in me a love of baseball and writing, and an unshakable belief in the power of holding your breath and crossing your fingers when the bases are loaded.

ABOUT THE AUTHOR

Born and raised in New York, PAUL HAVEN always knew he wanted to write and travel, so after graduating from college, he moved to South America and worked as a reporter. In 1994, he joined The Associated Press, working and living in Colombia and New York before becoming bureau chief for Pakistan and Afghanistan, where much of *Two Hot Dogs with Everything* was written. He currently lives with his wife and daughter in Spain, but visits New York as often as he can, preferably when his favorite baseball team is in town. This is his first novel.